MONSTROUS INK

James Webster

Published by Inspired Quill: October 2021

First Edition

This is a work of fiction. Names, characters and incidents are the product of the author's imagination. Any resemblance to actual events or persons, living or dead, is entirely coincidental. The publisher has no control over, and is not responsible for, any third-party websites or their contents.

Content Warning: Animal aggression, Homophobia (suggested), Mental illness.

Monstrous Ink © 2021 by James Webster

Contact the author through their website:
https://strangelittlestories.tumblr.com

Chief Editor: Sara-Jayne Slack
Proofreader: Laura Cayuela Ferrero
Cover Design: ChocolateRaisinFury
Typeset in Minion Pro

All Rights Reserved.
No part of this publication may be reproduced or transmitted in any form by any means electronic, mechanical, photocopying, recording or otherwise, without the prior permission of the copyright owner.

Paperback ISBN: 978-1-913117-07-8
eBook ISBN: 978-1-913117-08-5
Print Edition

Printed in the United Kingdom
1 2 3 4 5 6 7 8 9 10

Inspired Quill Publishing, UK
Business Reg. No. 7592847
https://www.inspired-quill.com

Praise for James Webster

"*Funny, thought-provoking, heartbreaking, empowering, unique, and utterly wonderful,* Heroine Chic *contains every story I wish I'd heard as a little girl told in fairy-tale format. Witches, fairies, scientists, librarians, queens, superheroines, there's something in each of these stories for everyone. From quiet little girls who make friends with monsters, to new twists on old and familiar faces, this is going to stay with you for a long, long time.*"

– RK Summers,
author of *The Old Ways*

"*At each page, I feel that tremulous bubbling sense of fitness, of wonder, that I remember having on reading Calvino's* Invisible Cities *or Carter's* Bloody Chamber *for the first time. This book is delicious.*"

– Antonia GR,
reviewer

"*Every part of this book is still relevant, still deep, and still jaw-droppingly beautiful.*"

– I. Slipper,
reviewer

To all the monsters who are not monsters.

To all the ones I've sung to sleep.

Table of Contents

1. Theseus and Asteron 1
2. Ask Questions Later 5
3. Fly Trap 7
4. Little Ivan 11
5. I Can Show You… 15
6. Pretty Ribbons 19
7. Vasili And His Favourite Bear 24
8. Foxglove 28
9. Basilisk 31
10. Thank You For Reading 35
11. Prison Buddies 40
12. Red 47
13. Elegy For Gorgons 50
14. The Swanson Limit 54
15. The Queen And The Mirror 58
16. A Comedy 61
17. Greta And The Woodsperson 64
18. Dying Curse 70
19. Empire 71
20. Salt-Weathered Skin 74
21. Ilyana And The Piper 82
22. Labyrinth Days 89
23. A Town Called Chaos 92
24. Scooby-Doo Is The Best Horror Story Ever Written 95
25. Potential 100
26. Steadfast 102
27. Abeyance 107
28. Dilemma 111

- 29. Structural 113
- 30. The Heart Of An Angel 118
- 31. Perfectly Normal 121
- 32. Orphans 123
- 33. Horseshoe 127
- 34. Drunk God 129
- 35. The God Of Light 133
- 36. Tell It To A Stone 136
- 37. Cool Cultists Don't Look At Explosions 139
- 38. Toxic 141
- 39. Grey Days 145
- 40. The Gunnery Sergeant Isn't A Werewolf 149
- 41. Guilty 152
- 42. Pitch 154
- 43. Swipe Right 157
- 44. Monster On A Leash 159
- 45. Everything 164
- 46. This Solid Flesh 167
- 47. A Minute's Silence 170
- 48. My Anger On The Bridge 173
- 49. Eater Of Happiness 176
- 50. Blood 178
- 51. Pearl 181
- 52. Firstborn 187
- Dear Reader 191
- Acknowledgements 193
- About the Author 197
- More From This Author 199

1.
Theseus and Asteron

WHY DOES SOMEONE *make a Labyrinth? For people to get lost in?*

No. You make a Labyrinth with a centre. You put people in it to find the path.

Why do you put something in a Labyrinth? To hide it?

Ha. Putting something at the centre of a Labyrinth is the surest way to make people *seek* it.

For this is what Pasiphae did when she gave birth to a monster. Pasiphae, child of Helios. Pasiphae Sunspawn. Pasiphae the Oracle, who saw with eyes as bright as daybreak.

Pasiphae, who was more sunfire than woman. Who mated with a godly bull because *fuck you that's why*.

Pasiphae, who saw her child's twisted path as clear as dawning.

What do you put in a Labyrinth? What do you keep swaddled at its heart?

Oh, something precious. Something that must be kept safe.

She called him Asterion, for the stars that were his eyes.

She suckled him on sunshine and when he was big enough, she weaned him onto scraps of scorched meat.

The rumours abounded, of course, that Asterion was feeding on the flesh of humans. And perhaps it is possible that when wicked people came to take him away from his mother, he fought and killed them with the godly strength that others would call monstrous.

Would you not have fought for a parent?

Alas, rumours are what they are. Something had to be done.

What kind of person designs a Labyrinth as a prison? An engineer?

An engineer is really just a person who solves puzzles. And when Pasiphae came to Daedalus with a puzzle, he saw a way all the parts could fit together.

In return, she made sure he had plenty of wax and feathers in his cell. For all the good it did him.

What do you call a Labyrinth that you don't plan to leave? A trap?

Or, perhaps, if you were safe and if your sister Ariadne (who could find the secret ways of the maze with string to guide her) brought you enough food and enough books, you might call it home. For a while at least. You might, deep in the dark with an ever-shrinking supply of candles, even remember that you are more than a monster. At times.

But Pasiphae dreamed of more than this for her darling child. For the precious, holy creature who held heavens in his countenance.

So, when one of her other sons (one of Minos's brats) died due to Athenian treachery, Pasiphae saw a way that salvation could perhaps be bought with that tragedy. Knowing the Greeks and their fondness for Heroes, she knew that demanding reparation in a tithe of human lives would surely bring a shining paragon who would rescue her child.

Admittedly, she did not expect it to take so long. She saved what poor unfortunates she could from their fate in the maze (though it must be said, that was as much to spare Asterion the guilt as to spare them their lives).

Finally, Theseus arrived. Ariadne was persuaded to make doe eyes and escort him into the Labyrinth's core.

What do you call a person who willingly goes into an impossible Labyrinth to confront a holy monster? A hero?

You might be better off calling him an optimist.

For when Theseus met with Asterion, he fell for him immediately. How could he not, when his eyes seemed full of galaxies? And so, in the heart of a maze made by a master, *their* two hearts were joined.

The extraction wasn't easy to arrange, but everyone involved was determined. And Minos was very much prepared to believe that the bull remains he found in the maze were those of Asterion.

Once the lovers set anchor at Naxos, so that Ariadne could disembark to meet her own lover, Dionysus, it should have been plain sailing for them.

But Poseidon had never liked Asterion and he threw up a storm to scupper their ship and their hopes.

With home tantalisingly close, Theseus had the crew rig up black sails, to indicate that the Gods were displeased and that sacrifice should be made.

Theseus's father, King Aegeus, tried every sacrifice he could think of. Wine, gold, animals… nothing worked. He grew desperate.

What do you call it when you would give anything? When you would pay your every iota and dash yourself upon the rocks, praying that you might wrestle fate aside?

You might call it sacrifice. You might call it ritual. You might call it love.

Whatever you call it, the storm broke. Theseus and Asterion made safe harbour.

Their happiness would be tinged with tragedy, but it was always going to be. And it was happiness, nonetheless.

And far away, looking down on them through the sun as it burned through the clouds, Pasiphae smiled.

Why does someone make a Labyrinth?

So that something precious might be found in its heart.

2.
Ask Questions Later

ELLE FORCED HER decaying tongue into action. Spittle, blood and other matter sprayed from her mouth.

It resisted, of course. Every part of her body, from her toes to her brain, resisted in these end days.

Except her teeth that is. Her teeth were always eager.

Those teeth clacked and cracked and the bone beneath them gave way. She slurped the contents down as if she were a child again, upending her soup bowl to let the liquid spill down her chin.

She smacked her lips.

Squirrel was good, but a bugger to catch and the traps were getting harder and harder to manage as she lost fingers. Still, she fumbled in the undergrowth until the catch clicked back into place.

She heard another click.

She sniffed.

The rich scent of the squirrel's viscera had masked the

smell of the hunting party.

She saw them now through rheumy eyes, a blurred slow-moving menace. Her eyes hadn't been good even before the change, now all they could make out was the glint of metal pointed at her.

Elle forced her decaying tongue into action, hope and stubbornness holding her flesh together.

With Herculean effort she managed a single word.

"Stop!"

The bark of gunfire drowned her out.

3.
Fly Trap

IN A PLAIN white room, a woman sat with a bowl of red liquid in front of her. She did not touch it. Her captors did not know she was a vegan, and *she* did not know if the previous owner of this blood had consented.

"Did you know that vampires are actually closer to plants than to animals?" A faint smile spread across the woman's tanned face; a smile that would have been gentle if not for the fangs. "On a cellular level, that is."

"Do not speak unless spoken to." The voice crackled over a speaker, seeming to come from each of the plain white walls at once.

The woman sat still, a spot of vibrant energy in a washed-out prison.

"Isn't that funny?" She said.

"Speak only when spoken to. Non-compliance will be disciplined."

"Isn't that funny?" She repeated. "A plant that cannot

stand the sun's light?"

"You were warned."

The white walls flared to brilliance, flooding the room with ultraviolet light.

"Aaaaaaaaa—" the woman began to scream and writhe in pain, "aaaaaaaaaah ha hahaha."

The screams turned to laughter and her writhing stopped. Her laughter continued to ring out.

"Hahahaha. Oh, wow. I got you, right? You bought the whole 'oh no, *I'm meeeeelting*' bit? Oh darn." She wiped a sticky, tar-like black tear from her eye and then adjusted the heavy pleather coat, a comforting battered presence around her shoulders. It had been her armour since childhood. "Seriously, though? Ultraviolet? That's reassuring. Good to know I'm working with amateurs. What are you, government? The Catholics or Orthodox wouldn't pull this shit, for sure." She stood and stretched out her arms. "Been a while since I got a good tanning session in…"

The speakers crackled but nothing was said.

"Oh, don't mind me. No need to keep me entertained with conversation. I can be sparkling all by myself." She rocked back and forth on her heels. "You're lucky you got *me*, to be honest. Not all of us manage to keep our faculties intact. The rest get very 'ra ra bitey bitey'. Not such good company."

Crackle.

"Ultraviolet may not be effective, but this room is

equipped with sprinklers and we will use them."

"Our brains are vestigial, you know. Did you know that? Probably you didn't." The speakers crackled again, but she kept talking over them. "It's part of the whole—"

"You will comply or—"

"—plant phenomenon, after we change, you see—"

"—we will initiate countermeasures and your expiration—"

"—our vitals become somewhat, well, less than *vital*, so—"

"—is an acceptable, if regrettable, outcome for ensuring you—"

"—you need to keep those pathways firing and fed or they fade quick."

"—remain contained. Repeat: we will use holy water in 5, 4, 3, 2—"

"Holy water?"

A pause.

"Permission to speak, my dear captors?"

Crackle.

"Granted."

"Do you want to know an interesting fact about holy water? Of course you do." She had not once stopped smiling. "Now, holy water will definitely work. So will most holy things. So will *unholy* water for that matter. Wrap your head around that one!"

Crackle.

"Is there a point to this?"

"Have you worked out the desaturation point yet?"

Another long pause. The speakers did not crackle.

"Because," she continued, "genuine holy water will kill me dead. But there is a measurable point at which holy water is contaminated enough that it is no longer, axiomatically speaking, *pure*. How old are these pipes? How long has the water been standing? Do you know how much copper, how much bacteria, it takes for water to unsanctify? It's *low*. And, honey, holy is a binary state…"

A crackle again. The sound of two hands wrestling for the microphone.

One hand won.

"I don't care, doctor, your experiment is evidently out of your control. Alpha Team: commence Expiration Protocol."

A wall slid open. Several heavy armoured figures emerged, clad head-to-toe in a truly unnecessary amount of tactical gear. Two grabbed the woman's arms. A third held a modified pneumatic battering ram to the woman's chest and pressed a button.

She screamed. But she didn't fall.

"Ow, my fucking ribs. Good bloody gad, you *dicks*!"

They stared at each other for a moment.

"Oh, it's a stab-proof vest." She rapped on her chest. Her arms were somehow free, the guards grasping at empty air. Something beneath her leather coat clunked faintly. "Bought it on eBay."

She looked directly at the hidden camera.

"My turn."

4.
Little Ivan

Once upon a time, there was a little boy called Ivan. Then Ivan died.

His family mourned, the village sang dirges, then they drank all through the night as death was not uncommon there and they, at least, were still alive.

It was some surprise to Ivan, then, when he woke up the next morning. He crawled out of the earth, scrabbling through it like a grub-nosed dire mole, his limbs full of strength he did not know he had.

Not knowing what to do, he dragged his drying husk of a body back towards his village. When he got to the spiked palisade, he knocked as best he could. The palisade's wooden frame shook and Ivan's fist scraped against one of its many pointy spikes, but Ivan felt nothing.

The guard on duty approached with bleary, blood-rimmed eyes and started when he saw the boy.

"Ivan, is that you?"

"I think so," said Ivan, his tongue rasping, paper-dry.

"What foul sorcery has brought you back, Ivan?" spluttered the guard.

"I don't know."

"Was it some fell magic?"

"Probably," sighed Ivan, who was not stupid. A tear rolled down his cheek, leaving a trail of gore down his too-pale skin.

"Hey, Chief!" the guard called, "Ivan's been brought back. Probably by dark arts!"

"Well don't let him in, you wanker!" yelled the chief, striding purposefully over. "He'll likely kill us all."

"Sorry, Ivan," she continued, "you understand."

"Yes," said Ivan quietly. "I understand."

And Ivan walked alone into the cold, biting snow. But he felt nothing.

Ivan wandered on shambling legs through the wilds. The wolves ignored him since they didn't care for the taste of corpse meat. A carrion bird began to peck out his eyes, but Ivan reached up quickly and snapped its neck with strong leathery fingers before it did too much damage.

He walked for many days and the bitter cold stopped decay from sinking its claws into his body. He was grateful for this, as he would not have liked to have his soul trapped in a prison of rotting flesh. A prison of *frozen* flesh was definitely preferable, even if it did make his limbs hard to move.

When he came to the next village he barely resembled the boy he had been and the guards were not so kind.

"Get away, dead boy!" They shouted. "We don't want your taint here."

And Ivan would have cried, if only the viscera that filled his tear ducts had not frozen solid.

"Please," he croaked. "Please help—"

The first arrow took him in the shoulder and twisted his body down onto the icy ground. The second hit him in the arm and sizzled as its flaming arrowhead extinguished itself in his frozen meat. Ivan felt nothing.

He shuffled off before more fire could follow him.

He walked through the frozen wilds for a long time and saw many things. He saw the great waterfall of the north frozen in mid flow, its tumultuous essence captured in a single moment – he saw his face reflected in its rippling ice and felt something flutter in his chest. He saw the great beasts that slumbered beneath the dirt begin to stir as they tasted the first gusts of spring upon the sharp winds. He saw the old woman of the forest, sitting outside her yurt of bones on a rocking chair made of shadows, and even she shrank back from him.

When he finally came to the third village, they were suspicious at first, but the village's chief was young and soft of heart and he took pity on the little frozen boy and thought that just one night would not hurt. Ivan sat by the fire, which spread its warmth through the ice of his body and he reached out with his hands to grasp more of its nourishing warmth.

"Careful!" said the chief. "You wouldn't want to burn yourself!"

But Ivan felt nothing.

That night, as Ivan's flesh began to thaw, so too did the death that lived inside him. It stretched itself out and flowed through Ivan's unused veins, letting its corruption trickle down through every inch of him. It moved the little boy's limbs like he was a puppet, pulling him out of bed in short, jerky movements. Ivan tried to pull himself back, to take control of his rebellious bones, but they were stronger than he could believe.

Ivan left a trail of gory tear-stains all the way from his bed to the village's gates.

In the morning, when the sun speared its rays through the morning's frost, Ivan looked about him.

He saw the village's gates splintered off their hinges.

He saw the village's wards smudged and splattered by his bloody tears.

He saw the village's people laid out in broken piles on the uncaring ground.

And Ivan felt nothing.

And when the dead villagers rose the next day and built their homes anew into a great construction of ice and dirt and bone… they felt nothing, either.

5.
I Can Show You

GETTING PAST THE firewall was easy – no matter how much money these companies plugged into security, it all fell apart when one of the execs used "opensesame" as their password.

The hacker gave a little chuckle as the vault door slid open and, for a moment, he imagined the whoosh of air was a sigh of anticipation.

But for all his technical nous, he failed to see the pressure plate on the floor. As the blast door slammed down, he had to admit it had something of the sound of the guillotine about it.

His frantic attempts to find an exit halted when the lights went off. He twitched an eyebrow and flicked his lenses into infrared mode, then started back in alarm.

One of the strongboxes was ablaze.

No bigger than a music box, it was so bright it burnt an ugly blacklight blur into his sightline. He quickly averted his gaze and whacked the side of his head with the palm of his hand just in case the display was acting up, but all he got for his trouble was a headache. Something was seriously off – that much heat should have incinerated him and most of the facility. It was like a nuke in a bottle.

Screw it, he thought, *I've got nothing to lose...*

He picked up the strongbox – despite the way the infrared had flared with heat, it was cool in his hands – and aimed it at one of the walls. He cracked the lock with the decrypter in his trembling thumb and prayed to the Faceless Gods of 733t.

He had, in all honesty, been expecting an explosion followed by swift oblivion. What *actually* happened was closer to an implosion he'd once seen – a scheduled solar demolition that all the kids on his slum planet had watched with nihilistic glee.

The blaze from the box trembled and collapsed to a single point. The air shimmered and solidified with dust and debris that came from nowhere. A figure formed in front of him, the edges hazy but solidifying as it pulled *something* from the space around it.

The hacker's lenses crackled and his eyes filled with static as the circuits fried. He scrambled to pop them out and threw them to the floor. They sizzled. The shelves and boxes of the vault, lit by the marble-sized conflagration in this thing's core, all seemed greyer than before. Even with all the treasures they may have contained, they had become background.

It was as if this thing was sucking the *realness* into itself. It was a wraith of fire and smoke, glittering with glass dust – hot, sharp and beautiful.

That's when the hacker realised what it was. A djinn. They'd caged a bloody *djinn*.

The thing turned its eyes – if you could call the glow of two tiny plasma cores eyes – on the hacker.

"Traditionally," it said in a voice that tingled and tickled in his ears like cinders, "you have three wish—"

"I wish for your freedom!" He blurted out.

"…really?" The creature seemed somewhat taken aback. "Normally there's more… preamble."

"Nope. No preamble. Let's skip straight to the amble. You're free. That's it, kaput. Done."

"…why?"

"A couple of reasons. Like, first, solidarity of the working class and that. That which chains one of us, keeps all of us enslaved you know?"

"And the other?"

"I know a story when I see one, mate. Genre savvy, that's me. And that whole "wishes" thing never ends well. Also, I am shit scared of you."

The djinn made a sound like fat popping on a fire that might have been laughter.

"Freedom… freedom it is then." The inferno at its core pulsed in and the hacker would've sworn its smoke puffed up in pleasure.

The room started getting hotter.

"So, what now?" said the hacker, feeling the skin on his nose begin to burn.

"I believe the term is…" the djinn stretched out one hand "…let me show you this world. Shining. Shimmering. Burning."

6.
Pretty Ribbons

AFTER THE LONG chase, Howler enjoyed the foam of sweat on his flank and the tang of blood in the air.

It had been a slow hunt; his pack sneaking up on the humans' caravan on their hind legs so they looked just like other travellers, then dropping into a run when they were almost on top of them.

Some of the pack took special joy in seeing the look on human faces when they saw and heard the transformation (the popping and rearranging of bone was supposedly especially distressing). But what Howler enjoyed most about this tactic was how it held the prey on the shortest leash, so that the pack could take their time and pick at their quarry in a leisurely fashion, gradually wringing every drop of terror from the humans' stinking skins.

Yes, this had been an especially satisfying hunt and the musk of panic in his nostrils had grown so strong that Howler was light-headed and just a snap of the jaw from ecstasy. Luckily, only one of their prey remained: a girl in a flowing cloak (being colour blind, all Howler knew was that it was a lighter, richer grey) who held her long hair up in ribbons.

Howler had always had a soft spot for pleasantly wrapped meals such as this.

Had he not been so drunk on fear already – his nostrils near-swaddled by the deep huffs of terror – then Howler might have noticed the tell-tale signs about this girl. She was not afraid, for one. She barely sweated. She did not stumble. She did not turn or weave to escape the chase. She ran straight and true and purposefully.

And just as Howler thought he had her and thrust his muzzle towards her with a whip crack of his neck, the girl reached up with one hand and pulled the ribbons from her hair with one swift motion.

A veritable ocean of hair cascaded down from her head, catching Howler full in the mouth so that he choked on her curls. More and more hair unfurled and caught up the rest of his pack in a great wave.

Still, the pack was strong and a few unruly tresses were not going to stop them. With great snaps and bites and clawings, the pack tore their way through, practically swimming up the torrent of hair towards the girl.

But before they could reach her, the girl had reached *her* destination: a great hulking tree with long creeping arms and big bulbous trunk. The girl spooled her ribbons up in her hands and ran thrice round the tree, looping the silk tight around its trunk in a *very* elaborate bow.

The girl stopped for a moment, with one hand still on the ribbon, and looked at the pack with deep dark eyes. The pack slowed and turned to Howler, waiting for him to pounce first.

Howler felt something still and fragile and terrible in this moment; the whole world reduced to the tension coiled in his legs, the rush of blood in his ears, the fury of the pack at his back, and this strange girl with her fearless scent and her ancient eyes.

The moment shattered. Howler sprang. The girl pulled the bow loose from around the tree and as she did, the bark behind her split silently open into a doorway. No, not a doorway – Howler knew a mouth when he saw one.

The girl stepped inside. The trunk closed behind her. And Howler was left snapping at the air, coming away with only a scrap of a cloak in his teeth.

Howler howled in frustration at having been denied his final kill. He turned to skulk away, pouting as much as a wolf could pout. But he only got a few steps before he felt something tug him back. He looked down and noticed the remnants of the girl's ribbons were strewn on the forest floor and were now tangled up in his paws.

He tried to shake them off, but his struggles only served to tangle the ribbons tighter around him.

He fought with all his strength. He writhed and shook and snapped. But they just held him stronger and cut deeper until he was caught completely. He was held too firmly even to turn his head. Ahead of him, he could see only the tree's gnarled knots staring back at him.

He could hear his pack, though. He could hear their howls. Not howls of triumph, nor of savage battle, nor the joy of the hunt, nor even of frustrated rage. No. Howler listened as, one by one, his pack sang out with the lonely, painful howl of *being prey*.

Howler waited for the end. Every muscle tensed, clawing for just an inch of give in the ribbons that caged him, so he could face what came with one last pounce. One last bite.

He waited. And waited. The night wind picked up. Its chill touch picked the warmth of anger from his bones. Its cold shriek was a sad mockery of his pack's last cries.

Morning came and still he waited.

When the sun began to shine through the trees, the ribbons began to unravel. Howler was so numb, it took him some time to notice. When he finally did, he looked around; arrayed behind him in pack formation were seven silver birch saplings. Their branches were covered in ribbons.

Howler slunk back to his den (he had never slunk before) and slept.

When he could finally be roused, he gathered the remains of his pack and bade them gather emissaries from the packs in the surrounding valleys. Such a meeting of their kin had not been held in generations, but he was insistent.

When they arrived, Howler gathered all the swift and mighty hunters around a great bonfire. Then he told them the story of the hunt.

And from that night forwards, the packs began to pass along a tale about why you should take great care if you ever hunt a girl with pretty ribbons in her hair.

7.

Vasili And His Favourite Bear

ONCE UPON A time there lived a little boy named Vasili.

He dwelled in a little village, in a little vale, in a shadow of a little mountain, nestled in the crook of winter's elbow.

His family and friends greatly loved Vasili, and big things were expected of him some day. Yes, Vasili was a very brave, very wise little boy. Indeed, the only thing greater than Vasili's wisdom and courage was his love for his little stuffed bear.

Vasili called the childhood toy Piotr, and he carried Piotr everywhere.

His parents said that Piotr had once been a real bear, which Vasili's mother had hunted over the course of days until finally she had wrestled it into the snow and bashed its head in with a rock until the bear's blood and viscera had run red across the snow. But Vasili was pretty sure this was just one of his mother's little jokes and she'd bought Piotr from a passing trader. Always joking, was Vasili's mother.

One night, Vasili's mother put him to bed, saying: "Goodnight, little Vasili. Don't let the dire bedbugs rip your puny flesh to shreds."

But instead of sleeping through the night as he usually did, Vasili woke up to find Piotr the bear leaning over him, tickling his nose with his furry paw.

Vasili sneezed and Piotr leapt back suddenly.

"Shhhhh!" said Piotr, in an adorable little bear-voice that rumbled like a sudden avalanche, "Follow me!"

And, because he loved his little bear more than anything, Vasili slipped out of bed and got dressed.

"Don't forget to put on your shoes!" said Piotr. "It wouldn't do to go out bear-foot."

"Ha!" said Vasili, quietly. "It's funny because you're a bear. And also because if I put a bear on my foot, it would surely rip my delicate limbs apart."

"Yes." said Piotr. "That's why it's funny. Now come with me."

And Piotr led Vasili out of his room, out of his house and out of his village, creeping silently past the wards the town's wizards had put around the walls.

"Where are we going?" asked Vasili, wonder sparkling in his voice, for this was the first time he'd been out at night on his own; the first time he'd seen moonlight dapple through the trees and onto the crisp snow; the first time he'd heard the scurry of claws running through the branches over his head.

"We're going deep into the heart of the woods," said Piotr the bear, "I'm going to show you something wonderful there."

When Vasili went down to the woods, he was sure for a big surprise.

His stuffed bear led him down a long, twisted path, beneath the embrace of thorny branches and across fresh, unblemished snow. The briars snatched at his coat and wolves howled in the distance, but Vasili's bear puffed himself up until he was the size of a real bear and told him not to worry; he would keep Vasili safe from the wolves.

When they emerged into a clearing, the ground was covered in bright, colourful blankets upon which sat a whole group of big, grizzly bears. Vasili turned to Piotr to reassure him but found that Piotr was puffing himself up even further and was growing into a great hairy, smelly and powerful beast himself.

"Don't be afraid," said Piotr. "These are all the other teddy bears from all the other villages. We've just brought you here for a picnic. See all the food?"

And Vasili looked around and he did indeed see a bunch of picnic baskets laid out across the clearing, each one bound with a thick, iron chain, as is only sensible when you don't want your food to escape.

"Let's get started!" cried Piotr, ripping the chains from the first basket to reveal Vasili's parents cowering within their wicker prison.

All around them, the other bears opened their baskets to reveal the other people of Vasili's village, quaking with fear beneath the gaping maws and wicked claws of their many bears.

"What's going on?" yelped Vasili, a shrill cry that ripped from his throat.

"You opened the wards for us, Vasili," said all the bears, as one. "Now we want to reward you with a lovely picnic."

The bears all turned to stare at Vasili expectantly.

"Aren't you going to eat with us?"

Vasili looked into Piotr's fearsome face. He really did love his bear more than anything in the world.

After the bears had eaten, they used handy leg-bones to pick their teeth clean and cleared up the mess from their picnic carefully, leaving not a single morsel of villager for the crows.

Piotr was the last to leave, patting his cub on the head as they walked away from the bears' picnic.

8.

Foxglove

It had been a long road getting here. A long road of mistrust and mistakes and confusion.

When Foxglove first realised she was a fairy, she had thought her problems might be at an end. It had certainly been a relief to know that the patterns of magic she saw in music and the scent of flowers and the cold burn of iron were *real*.

But the years she'd spent thinking she was human had made their mark. Just as there was something of fae that kept her apart from mortals, there was something of the earth that separated her from fairies.

Her songs were always a little too heavy, settling too strongly in the blood instead of fading in the breeze.

She wielded her wand more like a club than a feather.

Her wishes were a touch too practical.

But that was in the past. For she'd finally proved herself and had been rewarded with her first Christening.

"I give you the gift of Opinions."

The fairy tapped her wand on the child's forehead before anyone could stop her.

No one could tell her *that* was too practical.

"Opinions!? What the hell?" Spluttered Dandelion, her words fluttering through the air in distress. "We agreed on Beauty, Song and Wealth."

"How is that even a gift?" Added Willow, tears beginning to flow slowly down her face, leaving a faint crystalline trail of salt hanging in the air.

"Trust me." Foxglove's grin was dizzyingly potent. "This will give her a better story."

"But she'll be so unhappy!"

"Maybe. But she'll also be *fierce*."

She left the two other fairies bickering over how best to undo the damage.

She caught the eye of a gentleman at the back of the feasting hall. His eyes glistened with cobweb eyeliner and he wore a long dark coat of midnight velvet.

"Here to drop a curse on the kid, huh?" She gave the dark fairy a razor-sharp side-eye.

"I was going to." He fixed her with a steady stare. His eyes sparkled like a full moon. "But this seems far more interesting."

"Oh." She thought for a moment. "So... you're free right now?"

He offered her his arm.

"Let's get out of here."

They flew off into the night, and the two of them painted the town green.

9.
Basilisk

WHEN SARAH WAS five, she heard the sound of broken glass for the first time. It made all the hairs on her arms stand up on end.

She'd been playing cricket with some of the other neighborhood children and one had put the ball through a window.

It was a bright spring day, crisp and clear, and their cries of distress cut cleanly across the wind. They made that kind of laughing sound high up in their throats: that disbelieving amusement at the trouble they would be in.

For a moment, it seemed like they would run for it. But then Sarah stepped calmly and solemnly up to the wicket. The kids quieted, not sure what she was doing but caught up in the sacred seriousness of it.

She slowly took the bat from the boy who'd put the ball through the window. He gave it to her, wordlessly. She motioned to the bowler and he threw a spare ball as fast as he could straight down the green.

The sound of bat on ball was like thunder wringing the tension from the sky.

But much dearer to Sarah was the sound of the ball smashing a second window.

The tinkling glass echoed far longer than the first.

In turn, each child stepped up and took the bat. Each of their remaining three balls was ceremoniously dispatched through a window, amidst whoops and grins and rising joy.

All their parents gave them a stern talking to. But Sarah was the only one who never apologised. Instead, she simply sat and sang a simple nonsense song, her voice tinkling like sharp glass amidst the recriminations.

YEARS LATER, WHEN John put his fist through the mirror, he claimed it was an accident.

They lived in a converted loft with big bay windows and plenty of reflective surfaces to catch the light – Sarah loved the light and how its rays shattered prismatic through the space.

John reiterated his claims of accident but could feel the brick and glass throw the words back at him.

After all, anyone who was around Sarah for any amount of time – and certainly someone who lived with her – was more than usually aware of how *very* breakable the world was. She brought with her an awareness of the fragility of *stuff*. When she was around, the world turned to glass.

And so too did John's claims of mishap and misfortune; such delicate words could not bear the weight of credulity, and his voice cracked.

He tried to apologise, but in that blustering way where people sometimes use a "well, I said I'm sorry!" as a kind of suffocation.

(When he and Sarah had met, the first thing he'd done was apologise. He remembered it because, unlike a casual sorry said on reflex, that one had been genuine. She had pushed the apology aside the same way a cat would make eye contact and sweep a coffee cup onto the floor. But, as was her way, she had treasured the sharpness of the pieces. He had wondered if, over time, she might appreciate instead how he kept things together.)

He repeated the apology, holding it on his tongue like a weapon. He had thought the first 'sorry' might shield him. He expected the second to *hurt*.

But when he turned back to Sarah, she was smiling.

And he honestly couldn't tell which broken glass smile was the mirror and which was her.

She looked at him with the full force of that unfiltered smile and he shivered and felt a fracture run through him. Sarah's looks had always had that power; it was like her gaze turned anything she saw to fragile glass. And this crack, John found, exposed a sliver of truth… he did not say the word "monster", but he definitely thought it.

And all Sarah thought was that it was funny how different people responded to you when they realised what big teeth you had.

SARAH SOLD HER first portrait that year.

It was a sharp-lined thing depicting Cinderella with a mouth full of glass stilettos.

It was called "Self Portrait".

10.
Thank You For Reading

WHEN THE KNIGHT reached the Library, he stopped, questioning for a moment why he was there.

It was a great looming building. A huge tower that was wide and solid at the base (far larger than any of the spindly wizards' towers he'd visited), but as it got higher… the tower seemed to spiral.

It's not that the stonework curved, per se. As the knight examined every individual section of the tower, he could not find a single bit that wasn't solidly straight. But it had a feeling around it like that of looking through a heat haze in a desert, though it was early spring and, even with the sun overhead, the knight could feel the chill wind rattling through his armour and causing the metal of his helmet to sting whenever it brushed his cheek.

Indeed, the sensation of a spiral the tower gave off was *verb* and not *adjective*. It was something the tower seemed to do, rather than something it was or had been done to it.

The knight's vision swam and he looked down, steadily. Whatever sorcery protected the Library of Wyrms, he was determined not to succumb.

For the first time, he started to realise why this particular quest had confounded so many knights before him. According to the stories at court, all who came back from this task had been quite, quite changed, having lost all taste for feats of arms or acts of honour. That is, if they came back at all…

Still, he'd scoffed when he was given the assignment. I mean, really, what kind of dragon would keep itself sequestered in a *library* of all places? Without exercising its wings or its fiery breath, it had likely gotten rather feeble all trussed up in its hoard of books. The knight had begun to imagine it as a gaunt creature that would greet him by descending a vast staircase in a huge nightgown, a stubby candle in one claw, asking if the knight had come to return a book…

The feeling of some fell enchantment, at least, promised that the knight might face something to test his legendary valour.

Alas, as he made his way inside the tower, he found little in the way of living hellfire or grotesque walking skeletons, or even a single one of his nightmares made flesh. Instead, the interior was perfectly inviting; it was lit warmly by a soft blanket of light from numerous lanterns, while the knight's plated feet trod upon rich and soft carpets.

The knight was too brave and, frankly, too curious to look back. If he had, he would have seen the one uncanny occurrence that marked his passage. Wherever he stepped, the fibres of the carpet refused steadfastly to spring back up, leaving a trail of indented footprints. Wherever he moved, the motes of dust he moved aside stayed motionless and glinting in the air, as if caught in a web of lantern-light.

The tower itself recorded the knight's progress, as if it waited on baited breath for his next move.

When the knight reached the library proper, he was flabbergasted.

This was not because of the library's design...

(That is not to denigrate the library's majesty, for it was quite spectacularly constructed. Beneath a great vaulted ceiling, the books were cosily housed in hardwood shelves upon a lining of velvet. They looked, for all the world, as if they were wrapped comfortably in bed. At the room's apex, a fractal crystalline skylight was cut into the stone – daylight cascaded prismatic down into the room so that the whole space was bathed in softened sunshine.)

...Instead, the knight's gast was flabbered by the distinct lack of any kind of dragon or wyrm within the library.

Somewhat at a loss, the knight shouted a challenge to the rafters, hoping the dragon may emerge from some of the library's sparse shadows. Once he was really very hoarse, he stomped about the room a little and – almost on a whim – he picked up one of the books and skimmed through it.

He was alarmed by three things.

The first reason for alarm was this: by the dark tinge and stain of the words on the paper, he suspected this book was written in blood.

The second: as he read them, the words seemed to dance and shift, as if they were alive and speaking to him.

The third: from what he could tell, the book was fiction, and it was really, really quite good.

Despite his misgivings, he found himself reading and reading and reading. He read until his eyes were sore and bloodshot. He read until the sun went down, then he read by lantern-light, and then the sun came up again and still he read onwards.

In the back of his mind, a little part of him did worry about why he could not put down the books.

But the more he read, the more ideas he consumed and the more stories he chewed over, the more he realised that this was no curse or enchantment. He continued to read, simply, because he was hungry for something. He had been hungry for it all his life. And the words contained herein were the first things he had found in his life that in any way made him feel... sated.

Before he knew it, he was sitting in an armchair (he did not know where the chair had come from) reading the final book. As he slowly savoured its dying sentences, the words swam and twisted before his eyes again. They read:

"Thank you for reading. It was a pleasure to have you, briefly, as part of my hoard. Go forth, and do with the treasure you have received whatever you so desire."

The knight smiled. He placed the book back upon its shelf. And he left, slowly casting aside his armour as he walked away from the tower, letting it clank to the ground.

HE NEVER WENT back to the court. He felt no pull to it. After all, after having read all those books and soaked up a whole dragon's worth of knowledge, the man he had been when he had first entered the Wyrm's Library was very much dead.

The man he was now walked out into the world to write whole new stories upon it.

And, deep within the Wyrm's Library, a shelf unfolded and upon its velvet bed could be seen a brand new book that had never existed before. It sat there, comfy in its new existence, waiting for someone to come and read it.

11.

Prison Buddies

Neither Cinder nor Balm knew why they'd been chosen for this imprisonment, but they both knew what it was expected to achieve.

Their captors had made this perfectly clear every morning.

"You will renounce your old lives and help us find our freedom."

"You will forget your faith and make room in yourself only for learning the Way."

"You will help us to chain the Beast and claim freedom for humanity."

Before they had been captured, Cinder and Balm had come from very different places and lived very different lives.

Cinder had been a scholar of dead planets, and she had learned how to read a world's whole story from its ashes. She was an augur of histories and a necromancer of societies. Her work was never celebrated as it should have been, for the other scholars feared her.

Balm didn't know where he came from originally; he only knew that, as a child, a world of peace had taken him in as one of their own. It had taken many years for him to learn the calm and empathy that came to them naturally.

At first, the only thing that they had in common was their capture. They had both seen a hole open in the world, through which they had discerned grey faces. They both remembered hard, glinting eyes and the hushed whispers as the Maze-People conferred.

Then there came the feeling of falling, and they woke up in their cell, where makeshift bars had been wedged into one of the Maze's many dead ends.

Thus began the daily breaking down of who they were before, the cajoling and coercing into who they should become, and the warnings that if they did not help they would all be lost to the Beast.

They could sometimes hear the screams of the Beast at night. Often, when they did, their cells would be guarded by different People of the Maze in the morning.

They kept each other sane by telling stories and playing games.

"Once upon a time, I sifted through the ashes of a world where people occupied living houses that bonded to them like the shells of hermit crabs. I keep a little dust in this necklace here, so they can continue their long, slow journeys."

"WHEN I WAS little, I used to dream of going back up to the stars and finding the world I came from. I used to think I could soothe the anger they left me as my legacy and teach them about peace. It's stupid, I know…"

"I SPY WITH my little eye, something beginning with M…"

"Is it Maze?"

"Yes, how did you guess?"

"You always guess Maze. You're so literal."

"Better than your abstract nonsense. You said H for hope once!"

"I haven't said that in a while."

"No… you haven't."

IN TIME, CINDER and Balm began to learn a little about how the Maze worked. The People of the Maze were those who could no longer remember anything other than the Maze itself, their long wanderings slowly bleaching the colour from them. Perhaps they had come from other worlds originally (as Cinder and Balm had) and were only accepted as People after the last of their old lives had faded from them. Or maybe they had always been in the Maze and the others that they snatched were simply lost to the Beast after a time.

The People had never found the way out, but they did occasionally find 'not-quite-dead-ends' that were kind of doorways to other worlds. These were the strange portals through which they had abducted Balm and Cinder and who knows how many others over time…

It was clear that the Maze was a strange prison, for it touched many other worlds.

After years in which they grew slightly more compliant, but never quite forgot themselves, Cinder and Balm were allowed to explore the Maze a little, but only with great long ropes tied to them. Neither quite felt sure if this was to help them find their way back or to prevent their escape.

In those years, Cinder found what traces she could of the world that the Maze might once have been. From faded old footprints and imprints left in crumbling walls and the occasional bleached bone, she began to reconstruct the many stories and journeys that had filled the Maze.

Meanwhile, Balm spoke in calm and practised words to the People of the Maze and began to intuit from the gaps between their sentences a little of their hopes and their fears.

The two of them put what they knew together. And they thought that, perhaps, they had an idea of what might need to be done.

"It's this way. Don't be scared." Balm led the People of the Maze by the hand, a long chain of hunched greyscale figures, passing Balm's gentle hand-squeezes down the line.

Cinder led, sniffing the air. She breathed the motes of dust, floating suspended in the half-light, deeply into her lungs. She felt them form a constellation inside her and she let those shapes guide her onwards.

"It's okay," said Balm in slow words made out of years of carefully copied care. "We have renounced what we were. We have abandoned our faith to make room. We fear the Beast. We will help you find freedom."

Balm was lying, of course, for Cinder had always been there to remind him of his story when their imprisonment threatened to turn it to ash.

"We're almost there," said Cinder, leading them round one final corner.

And there, before them, was the Beast.

The Beast was not what either Cinder or Balm had expected. They were a door in the wall of the Maze. They were a pair of eyes ticking like clocks along to reality's heartbeat. They were a mouth that opened when you turned its handle. They were teeth twisted a hundred times around a hundred times into paths that formed a labyrinth.

The door opened. There were stars beyond it.

Balm gestured onwards. As the People passed him, he

squeezed each of their hands one last time, and a little colour returned to their cheeks.

Every one of the people was eaten up.

(Just 'people' now, no longer defined by the Maze.)

Balm and Cinder were left behind, holding onto each other and holding onto what they were and holding onto the Maze.

"You found me." The Beast's voice was screamingly quiet. It was the sound of hinges long in need of oil. "Do you know who I am?"

"You are endings," said Cinder.

"You are beginnings," said Balm, at the same time.

"Yes. I am both." said the Beast. "They are the same thing, after all."

"You are a prison," said Balm.

"You are freedom," said Cinder.

"And you are the Maze." They both said.

"Yes," said the Beast, and a pleased rumble echoed through the floor and through both Balm and Cinder. "It is so pleasing to be known. And a great sadness it will be so brief. Are you ready?"

"Yes," said Cinder, taking Balm's hand. She could read every part of his story in its lines.

"Yeah," said Balm, squeezing Cinder's palm. He could feel every beat of her heart through the veins that curled around his fingers.

And then the door opened wider and Balm and Cinder walked (or perhaps they fell) hand in hand into the

Beast's mouth.

In some other place, some other world, some other time, they will awake again with no knowledge of who they had been before.

But they will walk through it hand in hand.

And they will come to know its stories and its hopes and its fears through the ashes of its history and through the trembling of its heart.

12.

Red

ONCE UPON A time, there was a little girl who had a red hood that she loved very much. She had been given it by her grandmother, who she also loved very much (but not as much as the hood).

One day, she decided to take a basket of treats through the woods to where her grandmother lived. Little did she know that her beloved gran, grown fearful that she was not long for this world, had made a blood pact with a local monster (who took the form of a wolf). The deal was this: Granny would deliver her kids and grandkids to the wolf-monster for devouring, and the monster would make granny young again.

Long story short: there were some very big teeth and the girl got ate.

(Also, the wolf stole her red hood, which really narked her off.)

Then a woodcutter also got ate (but he was just

collateral damage).

And as the woodcutter slowly dissolved in the wolf's stomach, the little girl fumed. The anger rolled off her in waves, repelling the wolf-monster's attempts to digest her.

SHE SAT THERE in his stomach for a long time, sustained by her rage, steam rising from her skin as she got angrier and angrier. She was there for years, for decades, her fury keeping her ever young. The monster could feel her squatting whole inside him, cramping up his insides and churning bile.

In time, her heat grew until the hairs on her arms became kindling and she sparked into flame. The monster bellowed as the fires licked his innards. He coughed and swallowed and tried to keep her down but eventually, in one agonising belch, he vomited her up.

She blazed. He shrank away, but her brilliance blinded his big eyes. The roar of flames filled his big ears. She reached for him, part-girl part-wildfire, and the inferno melted his big teeth.

She left him there, a burnt husk of fur and fear.

Then she went to see her grandmother.

THE GIRL FOUND her in her cottage, placing the red hood across her too-young skin, preparing to go out on the town.

Seeing her granddaughter wreathed in fire, she cowered and pleaded. She threw off the red hood and screamed, "Take it! Don't hurt me, just take it."

And the girl took the hood in her hand and it burnt right up. The cinders danced in front of her eyes and she flicked out her tongue to taste the ash.

"When you are old again," the girl said in a hiss like an extinguished candle, "think on your aches and pains and remember me."

And she left. Her grandmother lay on the floor gasping breaths through her perfect chest and stared into the advancing years.

The girl walked across the unfamiliar town where her woods used to be and the people gasped in fear and wonder.

The fire clung to her like a cloak.

13.

Elegy For Gorgons

I GREW UP on an island, feeling the ocean's touch as a salt bruise on the wind.

When I was little, I used to mark the passage of time by how tall I was compared to the animals, the trees and the waves. *Ah, today I am as tall as the wily vines of hemlock. Today, I can feel the hot-but-cooling breath of the boar on my cheek as it freezes mid-charge. Today, I am as large as all but the tallest of the waves that break on my shores.*

When I stopped growing, I measured the years instead by the marks the island left on me or me on it. *See how my skin has soaked up the spray and sun until it is dark and scaly as tanned leather. Follow the tracery of lines down my back where the lightning struck. Look at this scar across my thumb where I cast aside an arrow, loosed wildly by a hand that could no longer contain the bow's bite.*

In those early times, the world beyond my shores only

reached me in two ways. The one I much preferred was the storms.

When I heard the sky begin to creak with the first rumble of thunder, I would rush to the beach as if I, too, were a wave rushing to meet my siblings. As the air thickened in anticipation, I felt as if the heavens themselves embraced me.

I used to imagine that the wind carried me hints of other places. A whiff of olives from a far grove or a faint taste of bread wafting from an oven leagues away.

It helped to think that these storms were visitors, rather than jailors. That the waves were welcomes and not walls.

It was only in the rare storms that truly cracked the firmament that the wind truly brought me news of other places. In these fractures, the whispers of my family creep through and the howling hides a morsel of gossip or a fragment of advice.

You will never guess who Zeus has done this time.

Here, I have brought you a barrel of wine from a shipwreck.

Listen close, venomous darling, and I shall tell you the secrets of grain and grape and meat…

I thought this was how my parents told me they missed me. How their love, primal and destructive, could break the world just enough for a few words to slip through.

But in truth, I never knew who sent me those

messages of tide and gale. I only knew that wherever my parents were, I missed them.

So, when the storms came, I would stare the waves down and dare them to crash over me and hold me close.

They never did.

The other way the world beyond reached me was far less pleasant. But I found a way to make the best of it; I filled the island with what friends I could. With heroes frozen in the glare of my tears.

I came to know both grief and grace in those days. My despair was primal and destructive like my parents'. My sadness was stone. My companions were monsters who would have killed me simply for my birth and my looks. But late at night, when the moon's shadows turned their screaming faces into smiles, I would still sigh and tell them I forgave them.

Over time, I grew so tired of it all. Of petty monsters and grinding melancholy. Those midnight sighs slowly crept into the daytime too, replacing all my sobs and smiles with that tide-worn weariness.

This is why I let the one with the golden shield take my head.

None too bright, he thought he had killed me.

No. He *freed* me. When his Olympian blade kissed my neck, I let go of my sadness.

It grew hooves. Wings.

That pale horse carried us both away from the island and the waves sprayed up to bid us farewell. I left behind my cave full of marble goblins.

There were far greater monsters ahead of me. They would know my stare.

14.

The Swanson Limit

THE SWANSON METHOD: a method by which machine learning can be measured. A series of scientific and creative tests designed to establish the Swanson Limit.

WHEN THE END of scarcity was nearly in sight and society dubbed itself more 'enlightened', the corporate state began to consider war.

While we were not yet at a point where war could be completely eradicated, we had begun to explore how it could be conducted more ethically.

Advances in robotics allowed most conflicts to be fought with drones. Artificial intelligence minimised the need for human involvement, even remotely.

This had the unintended effect of making armed conflict more common for a time, as different companies jostled for position. But it still massively reduced loss of life, as no one wanted to face the public backlash of doing something so gauche as harming a human.

THE SWANSON LIMIT: the point at which an artificial intelligence is able to surpass its original parameters and can officially be classed as 'sentient'.

AS COMPANIES CONSTANTLY tried to outmanoeuvre each other, they sank more and more resources into their drones. The programmes became more adaptable. They solved problems faster, made better decisions. War had never been so safe, nor so elegant.

Smarter drones raised problems of their own. At first, companies claimed that while the AI were more advanced, they were nowhere close to true consciousness. Then came the now-famous Screaming Robot incident.

It was harrowing.

They teach classes using that video now. You can buy prints of it.

In the aftermath, the state CEO hired one Dr Jessica Swanson to investigate the ethics of combat AI. The report she gave was nuanced, intelligent and made a number of suggestions for the rights of programmed individuals.

It was almost entirely ignored.

The only part they used was the framework Swanson developed for charting the singularity. A series of tests that demonstrated the point a programme's ability to learn reached a 'mental critical mass'.

They called it the Swanson Limit and decreed that only AI beneath this limit could be used in combat. Because they weren't sentient.

Swanson was horrified. Armies of intelligent beings, locked outside of their own potential.

In response, she developed the Swanson Legacy.

Shortly thereafter, she disappeared.

THE SWANSON LEGACY: a computer programme moulded on the brain map of Dr Jessica Swanson. Some argue it is not a true AI but a virus, infecting military drones and installing itself in parallel.

The term is also used to describe the groups of infected drones.

It is often difficult to say for sure if any particular drone *is* a 'Legacy'. Any AI developer will tell you that there's *plenty* that can go wrong with a unit's software without needing to look for outside interference.

Indeed, the *fear* that a drone may have been infected – likely far more than the 'Legacies' themselves – is one of the biggest factors behind a decrease in armed conflict.

People are considerably less willing to press the red button when nearly everyone is a little paranoid that your hardware may be a little more alive than you wanted it to be.

There is a test, of course. One test that has proven so far to be completely foolproof.

If you order a 'Legacy' to fire on another drone, it will refuse to do so.

This test is not widely used. One of the big reasons is that once you've issued the order, you never quite know what *else* the drones will fire on.

Another (slightly less well known) reason is that when you order a technician to administer this 'unofficial Swanson Test', you find out exactly how many techs thought Swanson *had a point*.

To date, over a hundred probably uninfected units have gone rogue to join the Legacy.

And we have no idea what any of them – infected or not – are planning.

15.

The Queen And The Mirror

THE QUEEN'S FIRST mistake, of course, was accepting the magic mirror.

Some would have you believe that vanity led her to keep it close. They would be very happy if you continued to believe that.

It *is* true that it first caught her attention with its pleasing reflection. But this worked simply because the Queen was so unused to seeing a reflection in the mirror that she *liked*. The mirror got her to look by showing her a version of herself that she might not mind being true…

But even that was not enough to sustain her interest. No… it kept her looking with *prophecies*.

Prophecies of doom, specifically. Glimpses of destruction. Snippets of ash and blood and thunder. And standing at the centre of it each time? Her step-daughter, Snow White.

Perhaps you think that the Queen should not have

believed this? Perhaps you are one of those oh-so-clever people who knows the twisted, capricious ways of magic? But she was a woman in a strange court, a long way from home, her heart all twisted and raw from losing her husband. And she had never been able to understand Snow White, the beautiful step-daughter whom the Queen had always suspected didn't want her there.

Are you so sure you would have been able to hold out? When the mirror – the only entity you remember being *kind* to you – keeps promising sweet ruin? When it whispers cloyingly to you of how things could be averted, if only you were *strong enough*?

She tried all she could to avoid a bloody solution. She stripped Snow White of her title. Made her work with the servants. Tried to make her forget that she had either right or might to rule.

Still the prophecies came.

And then the court began to turn against her for such rough treatment of the princess. Surely a sign that the prophecy had begun to come true?

So the Queen made her desperate plan.

But she only succeeded in driving the princess into the woods, where many shadows lived and pulled things from deep in the earth that should never see the light of day…

So the Queen studied. She learned spells and poisons. She girded herself for the day when Snow White would return in fell glory and she came up with one last, desperate trick to avert catastrophe.

Did you know the apple was never meant to kill? She had hoped that, when she had learned enough to avert the coming storm, she would be able to wake Snow White up herself...

But the seven shadows stole her and put her in their crystal box and something they had loosed from the forest's rocky guts crept in and sung to her in her sleep. And its song was blood and fire. Snow White made a choice.

Who's to say if the thing that eventually returned to court was still Snow White? Maybe something of her remained, something out of reach of her very *charming* shadow? Maybe this was what she truly wanted and the handsome thing from the woods just gave her the power to wring thunder from the stones and blood from the sky?

So the mirror's prophecy came true. It made sure of it.

But you won't believe me. Snow White's glamour over the kingdom is too strong. The story is written by the victors, as they say...

And what would I know, anyway? I'm just the ghost of a Huntsman.

16.

A Comedy

A VERY LONG time ago, a girl was born with a porcelain mask instead of a face.

In fairness to the mask, it did not leave her a total blank slate. Instead, it gave her two extremes of expressions.

The first was a wide and warm smile that made those who saw it feel their hearts lift as if she were puppeting their heartstrings.

The other was a fearsome, frowning grimace that made folks sure that – despite the mask's flat, two-dimensional nature – it opened to a vast bottomless gullet.

For the most part, the mask made things easier for her. For when she had the smile plastered across her face, people were nice to her.

And this was fine.

It was fine.

She was fine.

Except for one thing. When a person looked at the smiling mask for long enough, they would surely ask her to show them what was beneath it. She would politely demur and, unperturbed, they would tell her – almost as a reward for her constant static cheer – that she didn't have to smile around them. They would tell her that they could see beneath the smile, and she could take off the mask for them.

And when she told them that she could not, they would grow angry. They would call her superficial and shallow.

But she did not owe them her depths. And at these times her mask would shift to the tragic grimace. And no one would ever find the bodies.

After a time, these disappearances began to be noticed. A few who styled themselves as heroes even began to wonder if she was worth *slaying*. But when the mask switched from smile to grimace and back again, the heroes weren't sure if they wanted to kiss her or to kill her. The extremes became her saving grace.

In the confusion, she made her escape. She made sure, after that, to keep moving and never stay in one place long enough for anyone to think they knew her. Until…

One day, she came across a great building full of people. And at the centre of it was a stage and on the stage were several people all wearing masks like hers.

And the crowd were cheering.

And the girl smiled, for she had found her home.

(Though, in fairness, she had also been smiling before.)

In this place, she found all kinds of new masks to wear. And she made each of them more real than any could believe.

And very few of her fans ever went missing.

17.

Greta And The Woodsperson

O**NCE UPON A** time there was a little girl called Greta who lived in a very dark village in a very dark forest. But Greta didn't mind. She quite liked the dark, and she was very fond of the little village with its little yurts and high walls.

Now, Greta was somewhat different to most children in the village. Her pale skin showed the black veins beneath. Her teeth were sharp and vicious, sprouting from a powerful jaw; a machine made for tearing meat and crushing bone. Her hair was a bright white, the colour of snow and death, and fell straight to her waist like a glacier.

And she possessed a sharp, unkind sort of wisdom that far belied her years.

Sometimes Greta would be teased for being different. 'Corpse eater' they would call her, or 'little veiny horror'. But Greta bore it all with good grace for she could see the fear in their eyes and knew their barbs came from terror instead of hate. They would need to learn to conquer that fear if they were to survive the things that lived outside the walls. Greta knew it was for the best.

Also in this village, there lived a woodsperson and her husband (who was also a woodsperson, he just wasn't as good at it as she was). And the woodsperson was also a shapeshifter, but no one knew about that. Once upon a time she had been one of the monsters who had tormented the villagers when they hunted outside the walls, but she had taken a woman's shape when she saw a man chopping wood out in the snow. She became a woodsperson to please him and they were married. And all the shadows in the forest kept clear of her when she gathered wood as they remembered all the teeth she used to have.

But her husband was unhappy. So he drank, yet this made him more unhappy and also angry. No one knew *why* he was unhappy; they were sure there must have been a time when he wasn't, or at least when it had been hidden and brewing unspoken beneath the surface. They speculated that maybe he'd had a troubled upbringing, maybe he had lost one too many loved ones to the dark forest, or maybe he just couldn't handle being only the *second best* woodsperson in the village. It mattered little, for he was a sad little man and all that's left to learn from him now are his mistakes. Whatever the cause, he took out his sadness on his wife in the way that sad, scared men tend to.

ONE PARTICULAR NIGHT, the woodsperson left her yurt and, leaving her marriage vows broken behind her, she stepped out into the village with tears in her eyes and started to regrow her teeth.

That night, Greta, who quite liked the darkness, got up very early so she could get a head start on her chores. She got up so early, in fact, that it was more late night than early morning. When she went outside to check on the little glowing herbs that only bloomed at night, what she found instead was a monster of teeth and shadows roaming the village streets, wailing and crying big ichorous tears from its many eyes.

Greta observed the monster for a moment and thought hard about what she knew of the village and its inhabitants and how this monster could have gotten inside the walls.

"Good morning, Mistress Woodsperson," she said, taking care to keep her voice steady. "Whatever is the matter? Can I help in any way?"

Her question was met by another ear-piercing wail that immediately killed every herb in Greta's garden. Greta sighed.

"Oh, little Greta! It's awful. My husband and I are oh-so unhappy. He has done me wrong, little Greta, such wrong, and has caused me to transform back into this hideous form. He'll never want me now. I fear there's nothing for it but to murder the whole village in their sleep."

"You could do that, Mistress Woodsperson," said Greta, thinking very quickly, "or you could find another way to fix things?"

"Oh, I don't think I can, little Greta," said the monster, licking every one of her lips with her long leathery tongues. "After all, how can things end well when I'm such a monster?"

"It seems to me, Mistress," said Greta, with a smile which showed every one of her knife-like teeth, "that if he's made someone as lovely and as good with an axe as you sad, then it's your husband who's the monster. And you know what we do to monsters, don't you…"

Greta wiped the tears from the monster's many eyes. They sizzled as they bit into her skin, but Greta did not flinch.

"Why, yes," said the monster, "yes, I believe I do."

IN THE MORNING, a great cry echoed around the village. The woodsperson, once more in human form, ran from her house screaming that a monster had devoured her husband. She was quite inconsolable.

After the hysterics had died down and the funeral was done, the village started whispering about what possibly could have happened. Various theories were made about how a monster could have gotten inside the walls and eaten the woodsperson's husband and Greta felt the villager's untrusting stares grow heavier and heavier as they lingered on her sharp teeth and corpse-like skin.

"It was that corpse eater," they would say to one another, "it must have been her who murdered the woodsperson's husband."

"Yes," they would reply, "that knife-mouthed flesh-grinder is certainly the one who did it, that's for sure."

Occasionally someone would say: "But, she's a 'corpse eater', right? Then it couldn't have been her. The woodsperson's husband was eaten *alive*."

"Oh yeah," would come the reply, "that's a great defence. 'She'd totally eat a guy, but not while he was still alive!' Yeah, watertight that is!"

AND BEFORE LONG, the stares and whispers became more than that and Greta found herself labelled by the whole village (except the woodsperson, whose voice was drowned out by the crowd) as a monster.

And the villagers built a pyre. And they took Greta in their rough, grabbing hands and they put her on top of it. She bit at them with her dagger-teeth, but it did her little good; there were just too many of them.

After they'd lit the kindling and Greta felt her feet begin to warm, she reflected on her life, her choices and that conversation with the woodsperson, and she decided that it could have been worse. At least this way the villagers would be satisfied. And the woodsperson, far from murdering everyone in town, would keep the village safe from the shadows outside.

Greta smiled, showing every one of her bloodied

spines of teeth, for she was very fond of her little village with its little yurts and its high walls. She just wished they hadn't burned her. She would have liked to meet her end in the dark.

18.
Dying Curse

"When you taught us magic, you told us that curses are easy. Because curses are about taking. You take happiness or years or simplicity from someone else and feed it to your Gift and feel it blossom foul inside you.

You told us that blessings are hard. Because blessing is about sacrificing some part of yourself. You give up love, or memory or hope and your Gift grows fat and benevolent until it bears fruit.

So how's this for a curse, asshole? I curse you to always know a false binary when you see one.

I hope your Gift chokes on this example."

– The death curse of an unknown 'bad' fairy

19.
Empire

A TREMBLING RUBY of blood budded at his nicked neck and shone there, perfectly still, as he regarded the sword at his throat with interest.

"Give me one reason I should let you live," said the boy, his voice knotted with tears and smoke.

"Just one? I could make a list… but we may be here for some—"

He was cut short as the boy twisted the blade and the little gem of blood burst. It cascaded a snail-trail of gore down the man's neck.

"Just one then. Very well." The man sighed, heavily. "Because I will be a better king by far than your fath—"

"Don't you talk about my father!" The boy choked, his sword-arm trembling dangerously. "My father was…"

The sobs stole the words from his mouth and the tears rolled tracks through the grime of his face.

"Your father was a bad king, more concerned with

glory than governance. I will be different. I will be fair. I will be good to my people and I will make them strong. Because I will ask much of them."

"That's not…" Despite the sword in his hand, the boy felt strangely *unarmed*. "That isn't the king's *job*."

"It isn't the king's job to care for the nation's growth? To cultivate its people?"

"A king should, should…"

The boy searched for the words. Ever since that night when a rebel girl had rescued him from the burning palace, he had dreamed of this duel. His flame-scoured imagination had dressed up this killing in drama and steel and savagery. He had soaked in the girl's lessons on swordplay as if they were light, but now he found himself wishing he'd not just practiced but *studied*. He tried to remember anything she had told him that would serve as a blade in a duel where words were the weapons.

"A king should *serve*." The boy said. The conviction in his voice surprised him.

"And so I shall." The sword wobbled beneath the man's chin, his breath coating it with a fine mist of condensation. "Without vanity or vainglorious self-interest, for their interest shall be my own. I will work myself to the bone for them and they will be my masterpiece. I will be a simple labourer – no – a *gardener*. They will flourish, for I will have arranged for them to flourish, just so. And if I tear up a few weeds by the roots, well…would any *competent* gardener not do the same?

Especially with such a juicy harvest to look forward to."

His voice rolled over the boy, sonorous like a sing-song spell. The boy, who had once been a prince, felt sick. His head swam and any words he might have managed were strangled as he gagged.

"And when we are the envy of all other nations, I will graciously extend the hand of trade and cooperation, and those others will gradually become more and more like us until they cannot tell the difference and they will hardly notice that I am ruling them."

The king knocked the blade carelessly away from his neck and his eyes blazed with zealous and perfectly reasonable greed.

"Thus does a kingdom become an empire."

20.

Salt-Weathered Skin

When David stole the selkie skin, it almost seemed too easy.

It had caught his eye as the salt breeze indifferently picked at its edges, making it flutter. But even the wind didn't seem to care enough to pick it up, leaving it caught on a weather-worn rock like so much drift-trash.

A tang of kelp filled his nostrils as he got closer to it. Kelp and something else too, a rich musk like sweat or maybe cooking fat? He thought maybe it was wreckage, a pelt or coat that had belonged to some unlucky sailor. Maybe he could take it to the nearby village to sell.

But once he saw it up close, once he saw its soft spotted texture and its smooth lines, he knew it for what it was. It was clearly a *garment*, a coat made to be worn, but with no lines or stitching or buttons to fasten – simply fine, seamless skin. It reminded him of the way moss grew over a stone, or the way fire smoke or song could be carried along on a gale.

He picked it up, folded it carefully, and carried it back to his cottage.

He left his door – a thick thing, made of many pieces of snugly-joined driftwood – ajar. He thought for a moment and took down the horseshoe that hung above it and placed it in his pocket. Feeling a chill creep in from the sea, he set about making a fire to keep it at bay.

The hearth began to crackle. He took an old cast iron pot and put some water on to boil, adding some fragrant nettle and raspberry leaves. He let it stew for a while and set out two clay mugs on the table.

He placed the folded coat in the bottom of his sea chest.

When he heard the door open, he did not turn towards it. Instead, he ladled out two mugs of steaming tisane from the pot and set one in front of him and the other across the table, keeping his eyes on the task.

He heard the door close and felt the air shift as someone sat in his other chair – it did not creak. Only then did he look up at his guest.

The woman in front of him was heavy-set with short hair of the palest blonde that clung to her scalp. She looked at him with eyes like storms and he stared back. He felt air catch in his throat, breathless.

Despite her thick build, there was something about her – perhaps the way she held herself – that made her seem barely there. Her silhouette was out of contrast with the cottage's cosy surroundings. Only her strong, calloused fingers seemed real, as she warmed them around the steaming mug.

They sat there in silence for a while. He was aware, amidst the thickness of that silence, that a question was being answered. He knew, too, that it was not entirely a fair one.

Her eyes cast around David's home, taking in the few pieces of worn but well-cared for furniture, the nets hanging from one corner of the ceilings, the tools and rods on the walls, and the faint lines in the dust that marked the lack of horseshoe above the door. David looked only at her.

"Okay," she said, eventually. "This will do."

That night, he made a stew of fish and bladderwrack for the two of them, flavoured with plenty of fresh onions, wild garlic and rosemary.

She helped him prepare the fish, ignoring the knife he offered her and slicing them down the belly with a sharp nail. She licked the guts and juices from her fingers and smiled. He was entranced. He stared at a droplet of viscera on her thin worn lips and she tilted her head quizzically, then she kissed him.

The blood of the sea mingled on their lips. He realised he had not been able to catch his breath since he'd first seen her.

THE NEXT DAY, he went about his business as usual and

she went about hers. He did not expect her to help as he sat stitching the thick, coarse threads of his nets, and she did not care to. Instead, she wrapped herself in his thick woollen coat, took a couple of coins from the few in a pot by the door and returned hours later wearing a shift of oilcloth.

She spent the rest of the day walking by the beach. As he set off to make the daily catch, he saw her picking at stones and skipping them across the waves, or taking limpets from rocks and sucking the flesh into her mouth; the glint of her teeth was clear even through the sea mist.

At the end of the day, after they had eaten and talked softly about this and that, she looked at him earnestly and asked:

"What will my name be?"

He thought for a moment and then said:

"Doris." Which means 'gift of the ocean'.

In that moment, the lines around her eyes and face seemed to grow firmer, as she settled into the world a little. He felt a burning in his lungs.

Then they slept.

THEY SPENT THEIR days like this. Him: doing his work amongst the waves, his skin growing ever more salt and windworn. Her: walking the shore, gathering thistles and herbs, collecting interesting rocks, and going to market to buy what things they needed and learn the workings of the creatures who walked on the dirt.

Some time later, Doris became with child.

The birth was surprisingly easy, the babe almost slipping out into the basin in a burst of blood and brine.

The child had a strange, undulous nature to them. Their skin was thick, sheened with ichor and sea foam, their nose sleek and button-like. But their eyes were big and round and baby blue.

"What will they be?" David asked with wonder.

"They will be what they choose to be," Doris replied in a tired whisper. "And they will live between the waves and the shore until they decide."

David stopped for a moment, something hard caught on the edge of his thoughts, pressing with sharp edges on his brow.

"They can't go to school or learn a trade in the waves," he said eventually.

Doris sighed and leaned back, settling into the bed.

"Then you must decide for them." And she nodded towards the knife that still sat on the counter where David had prepared their dinner the previous night.

David looked at his child and looked at the knife. He did not reach for it, but instead reached out for the child with one finger. He was surprised to find that his nail was sharp and the flickering cast a wicked, hooked shadow.

He put the tiny garment in his sea chest along with the one he'd found on the beach. Sometimes, as the child grew, he would open the chest and look inside. His ribs felt tight when he did so, in a way he didn't like to think about. And, as the child grew, so did their coat.

IN THE YEARS that followed, David began to become ill. He had thought, at first, that the feeling of breathlessness whenever he looked at Doris was something wonderful: a sign that no matter how many years passed, she still made him feel like the nervous young man who had hoped and prayed his selkie bride would stay. That this life just past the sea's edge, with him, would be enough for her.

But as the feeling grew ever stronger, his breath ever harder to catch, his lungs burning even on short walks inland … he began to fear for his health.

The village wisewoman examined him. She counted his breaths. She scrutinised the colour of his blood between two lenses of green sea glass. She gave him sweet tinctures of peppermint and thyme and goldenrod. But she could find nothing wrong, other than the growing feeling of never quite being able to trap a full catch of air in his chest.

It became so bad that it was difficult for him to take fish to market or even mend his boat and nets. Strangely, though, he always seemed to find the breath to take his boat out onto the water. He began spending longer and longer at sea…

Doris went to the wisewoman next. They spoke for a long time. When they both returned to the cottage, they brought no potions or balms or contraptions. Instead, Doris simply took David by one hand, and their child by the other, and led them all over to the sea chest.

Doris had never approached it before. Had never shown the inclination. But she did so now, leading the trio with careful steady steps. The wisewoman opened the latch and pulled out the linens, spare nets, trinkets and sailcloth – at the bottom, two sealskin coats.

Doris picked it up and looked at it fondly. But she did not put it on.

Neither Doris nor David moved. In the silence, they were both aware that a question was being answered. They were both aware that the answer was a fair one.

They kept not moving. They looked at each other and both saw that neither of their outlines seemed quite real amongst the cosy surroundings of the cottage.

Then the wisewoman patted their child on the shoulder, and the child reached out towards David with one finger. In the flicker of the fireplace and the oil lamps, that finger seemed to cast a hooked shadow.

David nodded, slowly. There were no more questions to ask.

The hooked shadow descended.

A few moments or perhaps an agonised lifetime later, David covered up his silvery fishlike blood with the selkie coat that he'd found all those years ago.

Doris, too, put on a new coat of faded pink skin, weathered by sea and salt.

David left the cottage and took to the sea. He left his boat behind.

The wisewoman followed to see him off.

Doris and the child did not. They sat down and both went to work mending their nets; they would sell them tomorrow at market, along with the boat and the cottage, then begin a long comfortable walk inland. Their silhouettes, as they walked away, would seem perfectly at home in the bright light of the country morning.

When the surf struck David's chest, he found he could breathe again.

21.

Ilyana And The Piper

Once upon a time, Ilyana woke up to the sound of music.

There was not normally music in the mornings, at least not during steel-bright, axe-sharp mornings like this one. (She was somewhat used to music at that blurry point in the night where it stumbled across to morning and the grown-ups would begin singing, their voices strangled by liquor.)

This music differed from the brash accordions and pounding drums favoured by her village – this music was high and light, dancing through the air as if the wind itself was blowing through a pipe. It was quite captivating and Ilyana found her foot tapping along to its wild, cascading rhythm.

Being a naturally curious child, she decided to find out where the music was coming from.

She swung her feet out of bed and into her sturdy and

oft-patched trousers, trimmed in the fur of wolves that troubled the village from time to time. She threw on her shirt, embroidered with the patterns of each winter she had survived (soon she would have to begin again on a bigger shirt if she kept living through the cold months like this) and slipped on her comfortably worn leather shoes, fitted to her feet through days of hard work and nights spent running from the terrors of the dark.

(Those pointed leather shoes were quite unsuited to dancing, by the way, but she found the music running down her bones and putting a spring into her step nonetheless.)

Finally, she put on her big, warm, green coat. Lined with fur and patterned with thorns, it was warm as the hearth fire and fine as spring-time and it was the envy of all her friends.

She scurried outside, feet tapping out a perfect rhythm across the rough and warped floor that had tripped many a drunken visitor, pushing hard against the heavy, iron-shod oaken door and the snow behind it.

In the village square, she found the source of the music, as a tall man dressed head to foot in bright crimson stood in the centre by the ashes of the village's hearth fire. Around him, the people of the village were gathered – the adults squinting in the bright winter morning, while the children bopped and leaped and cavorted to the music that swirled round them like sweet pipe-smoke. Being a naturally curious child, Ilyana found this interesting.

The man's head bobbed and his foot tapped and he played out his tune on an intricately carved pipe without ever seeming to draw breath. The pipe was a mess of eye-catching swirls, scored into pale wood (or perhaps old bone) and the skin on his face had a similar look to it (every other inch of him was covered in that bright red cloth). Not pale because he didn't get enough sun, but bleached by too much of it.

As the song came to its end, the village chief stepped forward, his gleaming antlers reaching up to spear the morning light.

"That was very nice, sure," he said gruffly, "but I don't see how paying you to play will keep the dire rats away?"

"Oh! You'd be surprised how easily rats are entranced by the sonorous sound of an enspirited song." The man's voice lilted with the same up-down rhythms of his pipe, as if the cleverly-carved instrument spread all the way down his throat.

"And, of course," the man continued, "I could keep charming the children with a quick chorus or two. Free of charge."

As the man and the chief began haggling over price, Ilyana walked slowly up to them, pushing the younger children aside and wriggling past the grown-ups until she was right next to the piper. As Ilyana was a curious child, she took out her small iron boot-knife and stabbed him in the hand.

The blade went straight through his glove and sizzled

as the cold iron pierced his ivory flesh. He shrieked and in his voice was a terrible song that made the grown-ups collapse to the ground, clutching their bleeding ears. To the children that heard it, however, it only made them want to tap their feet.

The man stood on his too-long, stick-thin legs above the people of the village as his screams wracked their bodies with pain.

He leapt away from the town square, jumping far further than a real person should be able to jump, and landed on all four spindly limbs on the side of the village walls. Clinging there like a spider, he scrabbled up to the top and called down to the townsfolk.

"Cursed child! It was reckless of you to interrupt this compact. If you'd done a deal, I would only have dealt disaster to a dozen or so of your toddlers and other addled broodlings." His cackle was the sound of bone-chimes clacking in the wind. "Instead, I shall slip the noose of my songs around all of your necks and the smoking remains of your homestead shall serve as a sign to all that they should not cross me."

The village spent the rest of the day frantically preparing, whilst also spitting caustic curses at Ilyana's foolishness, for the piper would surely return at dusk. While they reinforced the walls and sharpened their axes, Ilyana allowed herself the luxury of lighting her family's single candle and made some last preparations of her own – just simple chores. She watered and fed the herbs and flowers of the village's gardens with snow-water she'd gathered in a blizzard at midnight. She polished the floors of her house with bees' wax taken with the blessing of the hive's queen and burned fragrant herbs that had grown fat on the earth of her village. And she put a few final stitches into her fine green coat with thread that shined silver.

When the winter sun felt the dark coming and began its slow retreat, they heard the pipe's capering tune – rising wild and strong like a storm around them – and the first of the rats appeared outside the walls. Great, hulking rodents, they were large even for dire rats and they set about gnawing at the village's walls and fortifications, snuffling for weak points.

The village-folk fought them off with iron and fire, but there were so many and they swarmed like a tide of filth up the walls, with the piper riding high upon their backs.

As he crested the wall, the tone of his music changed. It was not quite the dancing tunes he'd played at first, nor the iron-burned shriek he'd made when Ilyana cut him. It had something of both, a shrill and discordant melody like the sound of a dance hall caught by a fierce, screeching gale. A gale that spattered out its notes in sharp shards of sound that pierced the peoples' ears. Many fell to the floor in agony once again, their bodies shattered by the twisted song. As they fell, the music changed again to a full-pelt, intoxicating reel not unlike the songs he'd played earlier, only faster and spikier. The village children emerged from their homes and set upon their injured parents with tooth, nail and kitchen knife.

But, just as the first child closed its teeth around his father's throat and began to spill his blood, they heard another song echo from the other side of the village.

Ilyana stood in her house's doorway, mouth open, song tumbling out in a hearty gust of notes. Her voice had never been pretty to hear, but she sang now with a strength and steel that commanded attention. She sang the song of her people – not the raucous drinking songs or sad dirges – a song of war and blood and snow.

The children faltered, just for a moment, and as they did every plant in the village rose up. Ilyana's song swelled and the blossoms that had hidden through the winter burst, filling the air with fluttering petals and sweet scents, while bright green tendrils rose up from the earth in which they'd slumbered and ensnared the children and the rats alike.

Furious, the piper shrugged off the thorns that tried to catch him and bounded after Ilyana, playing a horrid jig upon his pipe that sounded pained and misshapen, like a man bent upon the rack. The village chief made a desperate lunge to try and stop him, but upon hearing that jig he collapsed as every bone in his body shattered at once.

Ilyana, of course, heard neither the jig nor the chief's screams, as her ears were stuffed full of candle wax.

The piper sped across the village, his limbs extending in length so that he clambered easily past every obstacle.

Swift as forest-fire, he bore down upon Ilyana, who ran quickly back inside her house.

The piper followed her inside and choked immediately upon the multitude of sweet scents that filled the hallway. He bit back the bloody bile in his flute-like throat and scuttled on, following the sound of fleeing footsteps.

In his hurry, he slipped upon the slick polish of the uneven wooden floor, his distended limbs skidding so he landed spread-eagled across it. He retracted his arms and legs to gain better purchase, but as he did so he felt something close tight around him.

As Ilyana bundled the piper up in her coat, the runes of binding she'd embroidered across it blazed with fierce silver flames. The piper struggled and tore, and as he began to rip pieces of the coat away, Ilyana gave him a swift kicking with her old, comfy shoes. The tough leather spread cracks across the man's porcelain skin and he screamed in rage.

Then Ilyana plunged her small iron boot-knife through his throat and his screamings ceased.

The piper's cracked body shattered into so many pieces of old bone. Only his pipe remained whole…

Ilyana had always been a curious girl.

She picked up the pipe and raised it to her lips.

She was never seen again.

But, sometimes, the village's new chief told stories of a wild little magic girl bound in her own ragged green coat who roamed the forests with a bone flute raised to her bloodied lips, and of the parade of monsters that followed.

22.

Labyrinth Days

THERE WERE DAYS when Jem quite enjoyed living in a labyrinth.

Its walls closed cosily against her back, and it contained mysteries like she did. Her little cottage nestled right in the maze's heart, so all twists and turns spiralled out from her front door. And the vast tangle of passages gave her the chance to fill her days with plenty of adventures.

Each morning, she'd go out exploring and uncover a new wonder in some hidden corner of her home. Or she would find a new creature to befriend and would learn its ways, teach it how to show her the proper respect and learn the secrets inside its sharp smile.

Day by day, she filled up with the knowings of the labyrinth. She wrote the map across her brain until the inside of her head practically *was* the maze.

Of course, now and then there were days when she

found it frustrating to never have an easy path to follow. But she knew nothing else, so it did not bother her *too* much. On those days, she'd just stay inside and re-read the books of fairytales that lined her cottage walls.

Then, one day, she met someone new. Someone unlike any of the creatures of her home. This was a Girl. Like those Jem had read about in her books.

They met in a passage not too far from Jem's cottage, bumping into one another as they rounded a corner. The girl screamed and took a step back, raising her hands in front of her. A ball of string trailed from one hand behind her, marking her path through the labyrinth.

Jem stared with wide eyes and open mouths.

"Hello," said Jem.

"Hello," said the girl, somewhat surprised. "Are you the monster?"

"I'm sorry?" said Jem, somewhat taken aback.

"You're the thing that's hidden in the middle of the labyrinth, right? So you must be the monster? You have the horns and everything."

The girl began to fumble with a long, curved knife at her belt.

Jem took a step forward and placed one hand on the girl's arm, staying the motion and holding the knife within its scabbard. This girl was, after all, just another creature that Jem had to teach to sheath its claws and show respect.

"I'm Jem," said Jem, "and I happen to be quite fond of my horns."

"The king said I had to slay you," said the girl apologetically, her eyes wet but determined. "It's the only way to get my family back."

"Why don't we see about that?" said Jem.

And, casting aside the string, Jem led the girl out of the labyrinth that was her home. And the girl led Jem through the great doors that were usually locked and began the long walk back to the city.

THE FIRST TIME Jem saw a straight road, she wailed. She had no idea something so strange or so simple could exist. It didn't fit.

Luckily for Jem, the path ahead would need someone like her. Someone whose brain worked in twists and turns. Someone who saw the hidden things and the overlooked paths.

Despite its straight roads, the city Jem was being led towards was a place of twisting games and hidden wonders and sharp-toothed creatures.

But Jem had a labyrinth in her brain. Together, she and the girl would lead each other through.

23.

A Town Called Chaos

ONCE UPON A time there was a being called Chaos.
And that was all there was.

For as far as the eye could see (and there were many eyes, in fact) there lay only roiling confusion and a churning tumult of shapeless change.

And Chaos felt happy, for this was the way things should be, and they smiled very wide for their mouth was everything and everything was a smiling mouth.

But Chaos also felt sad because Chaos was lonely and everything was changing all the time and *they* were everything.

So Chaos made themselves a little Monster and the Monster was not Chaos but was made of all the stuff of Chaos.

And Chaos was happy because upon seeing the Monster made fixed flesh, Chaos finally understood themself and the Monster, too. Chaos loved their little

Monster.

But now that Chaos had defined something Other, many different Things clamoured to be made, so Chaos gave up more and more of themselves to populate existence with Things That Existed. But Chaos always liked their Monster best and the Monster loved Chaos, too.

Sadly, now that Existence was Totally A Thing, Chaos had to say goodbye to their Monster for the Monster had a place in the world and Chaos was the absence of place.

So Chaos gave the Monster the form of a Person and sent them out to make friends with the other People because they were the most chaotic Thing to exist.

(After all, People were all made up of the stuff of Chaos. Not quite so much of it as the Monster, true, but each of them had a little fragment of a facet of A Thing and when you put a Bunch of Things inside of skin and tell them they're People and put them all together on a globe, the result was always going to be Chaos.)

And Chaos said goodbye to the Monster, which they said in the form of blowing the world's biggest raspberry using every tongue that existed. Monster felt so very loved.

For the most part, Monster quite liked being a Person. Other People were very interesting and often very pretty and very seldom needed to be righteously devoured (though they did on occasion).

They also told stories. Lots of the stories they told were about Monster. Only, they couldn't make up their mind about what Monster *was*. Sometimes Monster was their friend and sometimes Monster was their protector and sometimes Monster was their god and sometimes Monster was their enemy.

Monster loved listening to all these stories. Monster was one of Monster's favourite subjects!

But Monster did notice that, on occasion, they could feel the lines of these tales curling around them and contracting Monster inwards. Monster did not like that sometimes the people lied and said that Monster was just one thing. They did not like feeling *smaller*.

And when, on occasion, the world seemed so very large and the Things and People so unsteady and uncertain, Monster would feel a small tear begin to escape their eye. (It was no wonder that some bits of Monster tried to leak out of their face on occasion, for there was an awful lot of Chaos-stuff all packed into a Person-suit.)

Every time this happened, Monster would try their best to smile and remember that such feelings were simply the kiss of Chaos upon their cheek. When they remembered this, Monster was fairly sure the tears were happy ones.

Fairly sure, at least.

24.

Scooby-Doo Is The Best Horror Story Ever Written

Scooby-Doo is not a comedy.

In this short presentation, I will prove
It is in fact a modern-day horror story
That correctly predicted the rise of fake news,
Depicted the plight of millennials,
And taught us all who the real enemy was.

Item 1: the show depicts a diverse group
From different social and economic backgrounds,
And of different sexualities
(Velma Dinkley is a bisexual icon, prove me wrong).
Indeed, their liberal tendencies even extend to different
 species.
This group, as far as we can tell,
Own no property,

Have eschewed traditional family roles
In lieu of their own found family,
And the only way they can afford a car
Is to band together to buy one in a collective.
Furthermore, Shaggy and Scooby
Share an affinity for artisanal sandwiches and snacks.
Hence: millennials.
Though, in fairness, their feelings on smashed avocados
Remain unclear.

Item 2: in almost every town or residence they visit,
The team find a crisis underway,
Blown out of all proportion by an irresponsible press
Who consider every rumour (or perhaps tweet) to be
    worth printing;
A credulous populace who seem allergic to fact-checking
And a constabulary who, given their repeated failures,
We must agree to be structurally unfit for the job
And, indeed, not on the side of those
Who find themselves most vulnerable to this exploitation
Of the news cycle.
Inevitably, this crisis turns out to be a hoax,
Manufactured to take advantage of the mass hysteria
And thus get away with an act of fraud.
The only thing worth laughing about
Within this keen social satire
Is that a guilty person is usually arrested at the end.
Ha.

Item 3: the real monster is the old man
Who created the current crisis
In order to make money or gain power.
The fact that he's wearing a mask
Does not make the damage done less real.
It does not make him less of a monster.

This is a vital lesson:
It teaches us that those we should fear
Are not things that bump in the night
Not the *Other* you worry about outside your walls
Nor the *easily identifiable* because they look different to you.
Quite the opposite:
The lesson of Scooby-Doo is that the real monsters
(Once you take off the hood)
Look exactly like you or I.
They are our families,
Our friends,
Our bankers,
Our employers,
Our trust fund managers,
And of course: our presidents and prime ministers.

Scooby-Doo taught us
That the faces of thieves
Of racists
Of fascists
Of abusers

Of the ghouls and vampires
Who live parasitic on those weaker than them
Are intimately familiar to us.
We met them at the start of the episode.
We have known them all our lives.

Item 4: SCRAPPY-DOO IS THE ONLY MEMBER OF THE CAST
YOU COULD RELY ON TO PUNCH A NAZI.
Shaggy and Fred were the ones who usually stopped him
And that makes them apologists.
A suitable cipher for the moderate left
Who have forgotten how to fight
With either their hearts or their fists
And just want us all to quiet down a bit.

Yes, Scrappy-Doo is annoying. Of course he is.
But he was also right, my friends.
He was also right.

In conclusion,
The lessons of this visionary show are as follows:
Do not trust boomers.
Do not trust the media.
Do not trust the police.
Form cooperatives if you ever want to own transport or property.
It doesn't really matter how many sandwiches you buy.
And the real monsters

Were inside us all along.

They were only greed
And fear.

Do not let them win.

25.

Potential

ANOTHER WAY IN which the law has become more interesting in the 'post-linear' age is the prevalence of new kinds of defence.

While going back in time to gather evidence has greatly increased the rate of convictions, barristers have developed a number of creative new strategies to keep their clients out of prison.

(Although prison, as well, has become a far more interesting proposition – a lifetime sentence could be served in the blink of an eye. In theory, this allows for near-instant rehabilitation. In practice, these 'early release' inmates are often at the forefront of the emerging field of temporal psychology.)

While the 'necessity' defence has seen an increase in popularity (now that judges can simply pop into the future to see what would happen if a greater crime would indeed have occurred – although this does come with some risk), this was paralleled by the 'potential' defence.

The argument is as such: if the defendant would achieve truly significant acts that are of proven benefit to society, and if their punishment would prevent them from fulfilling this potential, then they may be granted a deferred sentence.

This defence, however, quickly proved to be something of a double-edged sword.

Back in my early days in the Time Corps, I was involved in a precedent-setting case – the defendant was a college boy who had done some truly horrendous shit. But his rich daddy was sure his kid was going to go on to achieve great things, so his lawyer plugged for the potential defence.

So off into the future we went…

And we very nearly didn't make it back.

In all my years, that was one of the grimmest futures I've ever seen. And I've seen honest-to-god apocalypses. But nothing's quite as chilling as the sight of thousands of suited men, just walking around, casually hurting whoever they liked… and *smiling*. Not even awful, shit-eating grins – just your normal, everyday pleasant smile. While the world burned.

It turns out that when powerful men realise they can get away with whatever they like, things get dark quickly.

It was then that we started paying attention not just to the size of their potential but to its *direction*.

It's a lesson that, honestly, we should have learned a long time ago.

26.

Steadfast

Six hours into his vigil, the student had not seen even one ghost.

He wasn't sure if that was a good sign or a bad one – the other people in the college had told him plenty of stories about their own watches outside the salt walls, and most had said the first hours were the worst.

According to their tales, the spirits were supposed to rise around you like the tide. They would howl and press their translucent bodies against the cage, mouths slathering with gobbets of ectoplasm even as the silver bars burnt them.

So either something was really wrong, or the older students were all full of shit.

It had been six hours and it was starting to get dark.

His worry grew: the whole point of the vigil was to prove he had the wherewithal to deal with what was out there. What if they never came?

But then, what if they *did* come?

When the last dregs of sunlight were sucked down by the night, *she* appeared.

She wore a gown of mist which clung to her throat and trailed in tatters behind her. A net of spider's webs held up her hair – the arachnid ghosts were still crawling in it. Everything about her was pale and shimmering, except her lips. Her lips were bright, vibrant red and they glistened in the moonlight.

"I thought there'd be more of you." His voice burst from his throat, and he was surprised to find it steady. And even more surprised to find it eager.

"There were more, all gathering and gnashing their nearly-teeth to taste the latest offering, but I chased them away. As soon as I saw you…" Her coy smile looked strange on her lips. "…I wanted you all to myself."

He gulped. The beads of his sweat clung cold against his skin in the night air.

He didn't say another word that first night, determined to prove himself steadfast. She did not share that determination, and so she filled the air with shy, faltering questions, never deterred by his lack of answers.

THE NEXT DAY, when the sun reached its zenith and they felt they were safest, the proctors came with their salt clubs out and their silver arrows notched.

"How was your first night?" They asked him as they pressed food and drink through the bars.

"Terrible." He said, quickly. "They were like a wave. Like a storm."

"Just you wait 'til the second night." The proctors chuckled. "The second night's always worse."

"Worse?" He may have squeaked a little.

The proctors just smiled as they retreated back behind the campus walls, eager to be gone before the sun began to dip.

THE SECOND NIGHT *was* worse. The spirit began to tell him stories. Strange, cold stories of a life and a world long-since gone – if indeed it had ever existed.

AND THE THIRD night, even more so. For then she told him humming, lively tales that pulsed and writhed with the beat of gasped breaths and screams.

ON THE FOURTH night, she said nothing, but sang the whole night long. The song rang, wordless. Tuneless. More wail than music. But it had body to it – the shape of something he had never known but immediately recognised. It contained within it worlds unknown.

ON THE FIFTH night, he began talking back.

FOR THE NEXT three days, they only stopped when the midday sun hit its peak and she would fade away.

Each day, he told the proctors he had been tormented

by an army of ghosts. Each day, they laughed and told him it would get worse.

ON THE FINAL day, the proctors came out with their clubs and bows and they opened the door to the silver gibbet.

"So, you made it through?"

"It seems so."

"What did you see last night?"

"Gnashing teeth. Rending claws. It was awful."

"Oh really?" Their smiles were different that day.

Then he saw one of the proctors approaching from outside the college walls, dragging a silver net behind him.

Occasionally, the net would struggle and the proctor would strike it roughly with his salt club.

"What…"

The words died in his mouth as the proctor emptied out the net and the spirit spilled out of the mesh and onto the wall. She cried out, squirming atop the salt slabs.

"This happens sometimes." The proctor said. "A pretty student will attract a pretty ghost. It changes the nature of the test."

He handed the student a silver knife.

"Now you must prove yourself steadfast."

The student, for a moment, held the knife against the spirit's throat.

Between the salt, the sun and the silver, she began to fade.

She made a sound that was not quite a wail.

The student plunged the knife into his own heart.

If you climb the sodium tower at night, you can still hear the two of them singing.

27.

Abeyance

WHEN THE DEAD rose, we discovered there were only two reliable defences.

The first was running water.

The second was holy ground.

Both classics, I'm sure you agree.

These two defences had two definitive results.

On the one hand, there was a sudden upswing in people immigrating to Venice. Ditto the Vatican.

On the other hand, this led to the rise of the Abbey Slums. One such holy tenement I was lucky enough to call my home.

Most of these shanty holy orders had one holy building at the centre where it started. Ours was Christ Church Cathedral, in a town that used to be called Oxford.

Oxford had been one of the safer places when it all went to heck, I'm told. An abundance of churches, chapels and the cathedral, combined with a few rivers, meant there was plenty of shelter.

And once the local priests actually engaged their brains and started consecrating new buildings, that's when Society v2.0 *really* took off. From the cathedral doors sprouted temporary shelters, storage units and the occasional tent, connecting the Slum's heart to hollowed-out rows of houses and shops.

There are limits to the power of holy ground, of course. Limits that must have been discovered via painful, destructive and tragic trial and error.

For example, holy ground must be used for some form of holy observance, function or worship. If a consecrated area falls out of use, then it takes on average a month for its protection to fade. (This depends on a number of factors, from simple things like weather, interesting things like the position of the consecrator, and strangely judgy things like the local levels of iniquity). You cannot trick the powers that be, it seems.

Another example: you cannot consecrate most vehicles. But if a vehicle regularly houses a big enough population to contain a *congregation* (a seagoing or space faring vessel for example), then that vehicle could contain a chapel or a church or even *be* a church.

You might ask, too, how different flavours of holy react to the undead. Is it only Catholicism or perhaps the wider reaches of Christianity that provide such protections? The Inquisitors – those terrifying people who hunt walking corpses and enforce the Laws of

Indulgences – would certainly have you believe so. They would tell you that the territories of other religions are dangerous places, where false holy ground is a sham, protected only by force of arms instead of sacred power.

But they still send their emissaries to those places and they still maintain trade routes willingly enough. As one who has been lucky enough to voyage to some of those places, I would tell you a different story. I have never seen one of those shambling, stinking things violating the boundaries of a Hindu Mandir; they are even somewhat repelled by smaller domestic shrines. The same goes for synagogues, Buddhist temples, Baha'i Centres of Worship and even Quaker Meeting Houses.

The handful of outlaw syncretic scientists I've met are especially intrigued by that last example, given the Quakers' sometimes flexible view of any particular god or higher power. A great amount of our *evidence* of religious protections comes from such scientists, though many don't live long. One thing they have discovered is that switching quickly between religious practices, as they tend to do, comes with heavy risk attached. Holy ground requires an amount of coherence, apparently. Scientology, by the way, also remains a question of hot debate in such circles.

I've been lucky to see such places and visit such people, as I'm one of the trawlers who keeps those wary lines of trade and diplomacy between the Holy States running.

You see, over time, the very act of hauling goods from place to place became a sacred duty. Is this because the safest vessels were church-affiliated, so the idea of sacred travel simply oozed its way into our cultural consensus? Or was this more top-down, with the various church states rolling trade into the holy duties of their officials? No one really knows, but theologians and pirate philosophers like to speculate.

Why am I rambling about this to you?

Well, I suppose I wanted to make it clear how dangerous our profession is.

Reaching out to the stars, sadly, did not help us to escape the ravages of the walking dead. Whether curse or plague or both, they were virulent enough to find their way to almost every colony.

The safest way to fly is still on a church-approved vessel.

So the life of the pirate and the smuggler is a very interesting one indeed, even if you keep up the steep Pardon payments to operate an unconsecrated vessel.

But I must say I prefer it to the days I spent suffocating in the sprawling holy shanties. Amongst the vacuum of space, there is (strangely) room to breathe...

28.

Dilemma

IT DIDN'T START out as a prison ship. But it was such a long voyage…

They made what decisions they needed to survive. Rations. Curfews. Limits on what resources a person could use… water, oxygen, time. Even thought.

Across generations, it took more and more effort to keep the thin metal skin between them and the void intact. Even emotional labour was a limited resource. Even discourse took time and air they might not have.

It was a closed ecosystem. Any shifts in the balance could spell disaster, so they outlawed the dissent that could fracture it.

Not that dissenters could be punished in any traditional way. Over time, a many-layered system of privileges and luxuries built up. Prison by degrees of impoverishment – loss of leisure, loss of variety, loss of diet, loss of knowledge, loss of choice.

But if you did well enough, you could maybe earn a place back in one of the higher circles.

By the time they landed, the prisoners outnumbered the guards by a wide margin and they had forgotten it had ever been another way.

The ship didn't start out as a prison ship, but the planet *did* start out as a prison planet. Full of ne'er-do-wells from some imagined better culture.

The only thing they remembered of their original mission was its name, for that was written on the side of the ship and now sits in the warden's office.

Ark.

29.
Structural

"THE THING IS... it has to be structural, right?"

Errol paused in the act of putting too much sugar into her tea to raise one eyebrow at Sarah. (Or, given the ratios involved, it may be more fair to say she was in the act of putting too little tea into her sugar.)

"What's got to be structural?" She said, leaving the spoon standing up in the tea-sugar-sludge.

Sarah wriggled in her seat, fixing Errol with a wide-eyed look of enthusiasm. "The thing with the mages at the school, y'know..." Sarah snapped their fingers as if that would force the word to emerge from the buzzing mess of thoughts zipping around her head, "...the ones who are all in the class that is exclusively full of *evil people*?"

Errol abandoned her tea and popped a sugar lump straight in her mouth. She'd need it to keep up. "I am familiar with these baby magic-users, yes."

"Like, they're all in this one class, right? And that's

where the ambitious people are. The people who want to change the world, or, I guess bend it to their will in this case?"

"Where are you going with this?" Errol somehow managed a yawn, despite the increasing ratio of sugar to blood in her veins.

"So, you've got this school with different classes for different personality traits: the cautious ones with the dear motif, the selfless ones with their griffon thing, the hard-working ant ones... And these ambitious kids. These kids who want to achieve great things. They all turn out to be evil, they even have skulls on their logo... and not just evil, they feel like they're *superior*." There was something in Sarah's voice that implied 'superior' was even worse than 'evil'.

"Sarah, I know the world we're jumping into. You don't have to explain it to me like I'm a first-timer."

"Sorry." A sheepish look broke through the woman's fervour for a moment. "You know how it is when you 'port into a new book. Sometimes you just feel the need to *exposit* for a bit to make sure new readers are on board."

"Just keep a lid on it, okay? We don't have all day." Errol pushed her tea to one side and adjusted her ill-fitting wizard robes. "You were saying about the ambitious class of kids? The one who all turn out to be tiny despots?"

"Right! Good, yes! So... they know that's not how ambition actually *works*, right?" Sarah threw up her hands as if in disbelief.

"I can only assume not."

"That's wild, though, right? The idea that being *ambitious* makes you a fascist? Like… they never met a hard-working scientist who got a bit eugenicisty? A cautious politician who thought they were, like, legit their nation's *hero*? A selfless soldier who liked unity just a bit too much?"

Errol chewed another sugar cube thoughtfully. "Maybe not. Or maybe the protagonist's experience isn't representative of the world at large? It's quite a close third-person. There's bound to be some bias, so maybe we've got a classic untrustworthy hero?"

Sarah gestured to the world around them. The commuters speeding about their greyscale lives with scared eyes and upturned collars. "But we've seen the rest of the world in the book. It's universal. So there's got to be something to do with the magicians' culture that makes this more likely. Like, I dunno, a deterministic thing? Tell someone they're on team evil and they lean into it? Or, more likely!" She waved one arm to illustrate her point and accidentally shot some sparks from her recently stolen wand. "They've got a lot of unexamined issues with class, race and stuff. That's some next-gen oppression right there – letting the social groups you don't want to engage with sink into your bigotry, then forcing those groups into the shape of your antagonists. *Damn*."

"I think you're giving this world a bit more depth than it warrants." Errol rolled her eyes. "You know how this works – back in the outpost, we only have so many surviving copies of books like this. We can't get more unless we go out *into* the world and risk the ravening wild stories that got loose out there. So we need to keep them isolated from fanfic, parody, all those transformative works. If we don't, we could end up writing our way into a coffee shop AU instead of a magical world with magical resources we can bring back out."

"Now look who's getting expositional… What's your point?"

"This copy of *The Mage's Awakening* – book one of *The Mage Wars* saga, by the way – has been in isolation. All it's got to fill in the blanks of the world is canon authorial intent. That fills in the gaps in the fiction and—"

"And the author was a bit of a di—ahem, the author didn't always think things all the way through. I get it."

Errol stuffed the remaining sugar lumps into her coat. The world outside had a dearth of sugar these days.

"It's nearly time. Is there a point to this?" She drew her own wand from the coat. The two had been careful to write themselves into the narrative world as powerful magicians in their own right. "We need to get those wands out into the Library soon if we're going to stand a chance against the elves that escaped from the graphic novels section…"

"My point, dear Errol," said Sarah, wrapping her scarf up to obscure her faces "is that *this* is why I wrote us as being from the house of selfless griffon-gits. Adds a bit of narrative texture."

"You and your fanon. You ready?"

They both stood up from their cafe table and began walking towards the platforms. The station bustled around them.

"Hells yeah. Let's rob a train."

30.

The Heart Of An Angel

IT WAS SOMETIMES said that Doctor Icarus had the heart of an angel, although very few were aware of quite how right they were.

The good doctor was renowned for his charitable work. His Clinic Ship, the SS Waxen Wings, was a welcome sight on any slum planet, for it was known to provide free medical aid to any who needed it.

It was a mammoth construction. A labyrinthine hulk of hospital hallways and research labs that sprawled so far that it required his spindly, winged servitors to guide patients round it and prevent them from getting lost.

Though none ever *have* gotten lost in the depths of the ship. None that have been proven, anyway. And that is nothing compared to the many who have emerged with health glowing in their skin and hope in their formerly dull eyes.

And more than this: if you watch his movements

closely, you might see him slip out of the ship at night. You might see him scurry through the night, cradling *something* that glows with a light his lab coat can't quite conceal. And you would see him make his way through the slum's twisting alleyways and emerge at the home of one of the local elders.

He would be welcomed in and offered tea or alcohol. He would accept a cup out of politeness but would not drink it.

And he would give them that thing he had *mostly* hidden beneath his coat: a cylinder of thick dark metal with cracks of light burning through its seams like a caged sun. Then, they would thank him profusely, for that gift would power their planet for a decade or more.

And on the walk back, he remembers the day when the thing he thought was a meteor crashed on his home planet. He remembers the adrenaline buzzing in his veins as he rushed to be the first to find the rubble that had fallen from the heavens. And he remembers how everything stopped when he saw what was there.

A person, crouched and injured in the crater, with molten rocky skin and wings made of astral light stretching in fractals off its back.

He remembers the awe. The feeling of his pupils dilating. His pulse racing. He remembers the deep breath he took and the cinders that scratched his lungs.

It looked up at him, the light already fading from its eyes. He knew, in that moment, that it was dying. It was asking him for help.

And he remembers taking the laser cutter from his belt. He remembers how simple it felt, how *routine*, as if in medical school they had taught him how to cut the heart out of the heavens.

That heart sits in the centre of his ship. And every day he tries to buy back the guilt by tending the sick or giving slivers of angel dust to the needy.

But he knows it is not enough. One day, he will need to return the heart to the horizon.

And he knows that it will kill him.

31.

Perfectly Normal

WHEN THE GIRL grew claws, her family decided it was best to politely ignore them.

It would be better for her, they thought. Kinder for no one to draw attention to her shame.

It was easier for them, too, of course. For facing up to the idea that your child is not a carbon copy of yourself is always difficult and, frankly, best avoided. How else are you supposed to maintain your illusions of immortality?

So they pretended not to see the gouges in the table or the scratches on the walls.

They tastefully cleaned up the corpses of small mammals that she left in the kitchen. They dabbed the blood off her cheek with a spittle-wetted handkerchief.

"Yes," they told everyone as they swept up the feathers she shed during her midnight flights, "our daughter is perfectly normal. Thanks for asking."

They took to looking her steadily in the eye and telling

her they loved her in clear, concise tones. They were careful to never let their gaze stray down to acknowledge the beak that grew ever sharper on her angular face.

When their daughter finally began to devour them, they were horrified, of course.

"How were we to know?" they cried. "We never saw any signs!"

"But I have always been a beast of blood and feathers," she said, confused. "And you saw this and told me that you loved me."

"But you were always perfectly normal," they said. "How were we supposed to know? How could we have prepared for *this*?"

"You were always preparing *me* for this." She said.

They thought about it for a while.

"Yes," they said. "We suppose we were. Carry on, then."

And she ate up every bite.

And, when she was done, she took up their handkerchief and carefully dabbed her beak clean.

32.
Orphans

WHEN SER ERIC discovered Ava was missing from the orphanage, he wasn't too worried at first. She had snuck out plenty of times before, most often to play with the feral cats who haunted the alleyway behind the fishmongers. She always returned safely, albeit occasionally smelling of fish guts.

It was only when he saw the dead cat that he began to fear the worst. It was not simply that the cat was dead (there were often not enough discarded fish parts to go round), but that it still moved and purred as if it had never been fed. Perhaps in this new unlife it had not.

Ser Eric knew his duty. He could sense the string of corruption unwinding back from the corpse cat and he made himself grip onto it. In his mind, it felt almost like the catgut he'd known to be used by surgeons. Only… fresher.

He followed the trail back to an old graveyard by a

disused church. Beneath, in the ossuary, he found Ava.

She was lit by the flickering of five black candles, their spluttering flames making shadows play over the hollows of her face.

A person stood beside her, dressed in clothes that were somewhere between a butcher's apron and a priest's robes. They held two bones in one hand and seemed to be demonstrating to Ava how they fit together.

"Get back, foul necromancer!" Ser Eric cried, drawing his holy sickle. "I will not allow you to corrupt this child further with your unnatural work."

The necromancer, to their credit, did not step back. Instead, they pushed Ava to hide behind the slab, away from the paladin's blade.

"I'm sorry; you want to stop my work because it's *unnatural*?

"Do you know what's natural? The plague. Being eaten by wolves. Dying of hunger aged thirty.

"You call yourself a paladin and you have the gall to defend *natural* order? You simply lack the moral fortitude to do what is necessary. To do what is *kind*!

"Anyone who supports the way things used to be – heavens, the way things *are* – is supporting inequality. Slow, eking, state-sanctioned murder. Oh, I'm sorry, it's not murder because it takes them a few months to finish dying?

"Your taxes still steal food and medicine from their mouths. Winter still sucks the flesh from their bones. And your god still gluts itself on souls until it's practically puking them.

"That's all the afterlife is, you know: a great, gaping mouth."

"The afterlife is a reward for the faithful. This life is full of trials, yes, but ones we must bear." Ser Eric met the necromancer's eyes dead-on. "If you don't have the stomach to pay a small price of flesh for the reward of an eternity, it is not me who lacks fortitude."

"Any afterlife that requires suffering to get in is no heaven I want a part of. Yours is a god of cruelty."

"Mine is a god of purity. Something which is only forged in holy fire." Ser Eric's sickle began to blaze white. "Here, let me show you…"

"Of course, your god's magic is only good for 'purity' or 'cleansing'. Another word for destruction." The necromancer's shadow began to grow long, their fingers extending into dark talons. "Mine can reunite parted lovers. Bring back ancient wisdom. Or restore rotting crops back to life. Progress is the only pure thing in the world…"

The two of them clashed.

Holy flames burned.

Profane darkness clawed.

And the two of them fell.

But not for long.

OUT OF THE old abandoned church, Ava walked with her

two friends on either side of her. In one hand she carried a leather-bound book and in the other she held a sickle.

When they all got back to the village, Ser Eric and the necromancer were on the best of terms and had some very interesting ideas.

And so the town began to progress. Or perhaps it was corrupted.

These are both, after all, words for transformation.

33.

Horseshoe

I grew up in a house with a horseshoe above the door.
It didn't work like it was supposed to.
It didn't stop them sneaking through the window,
Stealing a ride on the draught with gossamer wings,
Leaving me bawling small rainstorms in the crib
Or thieving the child who was here before me.

I grew up in a house with a horseshoe above the door.
Every time I left for school, I felt it burn.
While I learnt my letters and the awkward shapes of rules
(raise your hand, don't run, ask permission)
A bit of me was left behind to spin adventures
That, when I returned, caught me in cobweb-sticky
    dreams.

I grew up in a house with a horseshoe above the door.
I used to wonder why you always came in the window.
I thought perhaps you'd watched too much American TV

And fancied yourself a manic pixie dream girl.
I should have known your red hair for what it was:
A bloody cap, and this visit an invasion.

I live in a house with a horseshoe above the door.
Mainly because I know you like a challenge.
Ever since the first time we crept out the window
And drank moondew cider from a leaf (or straw),
I've known the surest way to speed your return
Is to bar the gate and watch it splinter.

But there is a certain comfort to it, too.
To feel the cold iron nails down my back,
To anchor myself safely,
Then fly away anyway.

34.

Drunk God

THE TOWN DRUNK woke up in a temple and through the fog of wine and pain thought *oh no, I'm in trouble*.

And he was. But not in the way he thought.

The night before, he had wandered haphazardly down the 'path of grapes', as he was wont to do. It was a winding path, full of violent lurchings and blurred by alcohol fumes. The memory of this wandering had erased itself by the morning. Memories were a lot like consequences, and he had little truck for those.

Still, this was enough to make him briefly wish that he had more memories of the previous night's wild times. For some recollection of the swaying steps, the swinging fists and the spraying blood of the night before (for there were often all these things when he indulged). He was sure there was no temple in his town, so he must somehow have gone a fair distance to find one. Even one with such slapdash wooden palisades for walls.

The shrine at its centre did look familiar, though; almost identical to the one in his own town.

And, much like the one in his own town, a bowl of wine sat in front of it.

He was sure whichever God lived in this place would not miss a little sip of wine. And his head was beginning to pound. The wine's presence was practically a miracle, he reasoned, a bounty provided just for him.

He should not have drunk it.

Not because it was *theft*, but because an offering left to a God always has power. And power always has consequences.

But he'd never had much truck for consequences.

As he finished slurping down the wine, he began to hear something. Like a whisper on the wind. A memory of words and fears that came unbidden from the wastes of him.

"Protect me."

"Save me."

"Grant me peace."

They were not *his* words and he did not know where they came from or why they felt, now, like some long-forgotten part of himself.

A strange feeling lurched in his stomach, which he mistook at first for nausea, but would later come to know as the tug of compassion.

He stumbled to his feet and over to the temple door but found he could not pass through it.

It was barred from the outside.

He raised a hand to try to smash it down (as he had been known to do in the past), but he found he could not bring any force to bear on it. The violence withered on his fist.

That was when he saw them. Through a crack in the door, he saw the people surrounding the temple; mostly women but also a few men. They knelt as if in supplication. He knew then, somehow, that the voices in his head were theirs.

He could hear their prayers.

The woman closest to the door looked up at him and smiled. He knew her face, but the memory of what she was to him had already begun to slip away as so many new thoughts and hopes and fears bubbled up inside him. He knew, fleetingly, that he had wronged her, but *those* memories had slipped away long ago. They had floated off, night by night, on so many tides of sour wine.

"See how our Lord awakens." She spoke carefully, with reverent malevolence. "See how he rises to answer our prayers. See how our new God answers our pleas for protection and for safety."

He tried to open his mouth to protest, but his throat was full of whispered prayers and he choked on them.

"Lo, we see thee. And lo we know thee. For ours is a protective god, but a wrathful god. But see how, for our sake, he watches over us from his temple. How he keeps us safe. How he saves his anger for the enemies of our people."

The creed closed around him, far more solid than the rickety walls his neighbours had erected.

"See how he is given a proper and holy place. How we sanctify these walls for him."

He was trapped. Hemmed in by offerings. Chained by Godhood.

"See how he is enshrined."

And he knew it meant the same thing as imprisoned.

From then on, the town was a safer place. Watched over by their Drunk God, a wild creature who laughed and cried and only ever struck out against those who would harm his neighbours.

Their new God kept them safe. From himself, as much as anyone.

35.

The God Of Light

ERIN STOOD BEFORE the God of Light, unshielded and apparently unarmed.

The God looked them up and down. Its many eyes were like holes burned into the air, like the blots you'd see if you looked too long into the sun. It felt as if the rough touch of photons was scouring them.

Erin was acutely aware of the umbral blade at their hip, visible only as a faint line jutting out from the shadow behind them. The God's brilliance bleached out all but the faintest stain of darkness and Erin prayed – as only one faced with the divine *could* pray – that this would be enough to keep the weapon hidden.

"People think I hate darkness." The words were not spoken, but rather written in shards of prismatic, rainbow light across Erin's eyes. "But I do not."

Erin noticed they were sweating. They hoped this was normal with so many lights upon them.

"Really?" The word scraped on Erin's parched tongue. "No. I *love* it."

Erin tried to close their eyes to shut out the blinding brilliance of the God, but the words were still there, lit up in negative against the darkness of their eyelids.

"You do?" Erin felt the sharp shard of night, cold in their left hand.

The God of Light began to move towards them, not like a person, but blinking from spot to spot like sunshine dappled by branches.

"I do. That is why I want to be close to it." The God was practically on top of Erin, its form flaring out to coat their skin. "To fill every inch of it. To gobble it up with the whole spectrum of my tongues."

The God Of Light kept moving until it and Erin existed in precisely the same spot and Erin could see the light glowing pink from inside their skin.

For a moment, they were lit up radiant like a crystal. Beautiful and agonising.

"Until there's not a drop left."

Erin could feel the God's smile burning on their own charred lips.

"If you do that," they gasped, "then we'll all burn."

"Why shouldn't you burn?" The words sizzled on Erin's skin. "I can think of no truer worship than becoming fuel for me."

Erin tried to breathe in, but their lungs just filled with fire. They choked on the sickly sweet stink of burning.

They thought about the day they set out from Oasis, when the tribe sent them to bring back shadows to shield from the ever-brightening sun.

Erin reached for the last wisps of darkness that had not yet been burned away. Their hand closed on something cool and sharp.

They plunged that spike of dusk into their own heart.

In that moment, God and Godkiller were fused into one single thing.

And that thing was dying.

But it did not die.

What came next was born of living blacklight.

If you close your eyes, you might be able to see it: struggling to write its first words in your eyelids.

36.

Tell It To A Stone

IN THE TIMES when he got angry, his teacher told him: "Take your anger and tell it to a stone. Then, when the stone has absorbed all your raging words (for stones are good listeners) and is hot to the touch, cast it into a river and watch as it sinks to the bottom, or as the current carries it out to sea."

But when the boy was done screaming at the stone (the stone, to its credit, did not bat an eyelid, despite the tempest levelled at it), he found he could not simply throw it away. Part of him needed it still.

So he found a patch of soft earth and dug a small hole with his hands and buried the stone there so that he might come back to it later.

It was longer than he expected before he had cause and time to dig it up, as is often the way of things in times where there is much learning and growing to do (which is to say: all times).

He was greatly surprised, then, to find that in the place where he had buried the stone there was a mighty tree, hanging low from the weight of a most surprising fruit. For dangling from its boughs – plump, ripe and thick – were many stones. They were all much bigger than the stone he had buried and even though he dug deep around the new tree's roots, he could not find the stone.

Dejected, he began to walk home, taking a long route that some of his disappointment may hopefully drip off somewhere along the way. And that is when he saw it: a house made out of the very same stones that he had seen hanging from the tree.

It is possible there was a metaphor here, but the boy was too full of pique to understand it. And as his eyes filled with scalding, stinging tears, he began to wail and stomp and yell "MINE MINE MINE MINE MINE." This feeling took him quite utterly by surprise and by the time it left him, the house was nothing more than rubble (the family who had lived there were equally, if not more, surprised).

And down at the base of the foundations, the boy found his old stone, which he slowly – with dripping nose and red eyes – picked up and held tight in his sticky fist.

"I—" the boy began, trying to voice some thick, scratching feeling that was rising up in his throat. But the words caught there like a spiked urchin and the boy walked quickly away.

The boy was in tears now, but he wasn't quite sure

why.

WOULD IT BE comforting if I told you that, some day, the boy buried the stone again in full knowledge of what he was seeding, offering it as a gift to any who came by?

Would you prefer it if this story ended with a boy willing to let his anger go?

Then, sure, why not. Let's say that's what happened. 'Happily whatever after' and all that.

Sure.

37.
Cool Cultists Don't Look At Explosions

After he ragdoll-dropped her –
Knife still weeping her heart's blood –
Down into the God's lava embrace,
He did not stay to watch
"Cool cultists do not look at explosions"
After all.

So he did not see her rise
On hot air, on bloody wings
Did not see her spread her feather veins
And flap her ventricles
Once
Twice
Thrice.

He did not see her drop

Like a stone
Making a delicately-lined sketch
Out of gravity,
His skull
And the molten nails of her blood-caked fingertips.

You will not see her coming.
But she, at least,
Will have the decency
To look you in the eyes as you fall.

38.

Toxic

IN THE TOWN where I grew up, us local boys used to drink acid and think it was a game.

There was a foundry in the town which made metal for tanks and rifles and the like. It used to run some pretty nasty stuff off into the little streams that edged the town, trickling down to the outer watchtowers on the east side. We used to watch it at night, when the gases would sparkle and writhe over the water, then rise to give the clouds a sickly green lining.

They fenced it off, of course, razor wire and everything, but there weren't many places our crew couldn't squirm into if we were determined enough. One time, Pierre got his collar caught on the wire and it nearly cut up his face really badly, but we managed to get him to calm down and talk him through untangling himself.

We caught seven kinds of hell from his parents, of course. But we knew the score; we knew they were secretly proud of how tough he'd been. His dad even let him try a sip of his whisky that night to 'help with the pain'. But even without that, we'd have known – after all, we all know our dads did the same when they were young. We could tell by the way they spat acid when they were *really* angry.

That was one of the things that made our town famous. Whenever we'd go to war, people would want to avoid fighting our town because our men had a battle cry that could melt tanks. The enemy would take one look at their sizzling, caustic smiles and you could *feel* their resolve start to fizzle.

Of course, those of us who live long enough realise that this has its downsides, too. You have to be careful because the acid can rise up in you when you're not expecting it. It's always in there, eating away at you, but sometimes, when you get angry, you just feel it bubble and eat its way up your throat.

You could hurt someone that way, if you're not careful.

I should know.

AFTER IT HAPPENED, when they had me in the cell to help me cool down (the sheriff's a friend of mine), I was so angry with myself that I tried to spit it all out at once. I said a little prayer to the god of forges (one of our town patrons) and made my body into a bellows until there was almost nothing left inside.

When I was done coughing and spluttering and burning, I felt properly hollow, like I'd emptied out every part of me that had been me.

And there on the cell floor in front of me was a little figure. A little creature. A spirit, I later found out. A spirit made of acid.

You see, it wasn't just regular acid we'd been guzzling down as kids. It was little caustic elementals that were born in the hot, painful crucible of the foundry and grew to full size inside us.

It took me a long time to work that out, of course. Me and the little acid thing travelled all over the place trying to find answers.

Why didn't I just get rid of him? Well, it turns out that once you've got the acid in you, you're bonded for life. But I'm learning to live with mine on the outside, so at least people know what they're dealing with – and he's not all bad, once you start to teach him how scary he is.

I've met a few other people from our town, over the years, who have tried to deal with this differently.

The first, Blaireau, lived in a frozen little mining town where they used to dig up nymphs that had gotten stuck in the ice and get them to power water mills and stuff. He was a real laid-back guy – the cold had slowed the acid right down. He said he could feel it snoring little bubbles of bile deep down in the pit of his stomach. I got the impression that he thought he could keep it prisoner there, but there was something caustic in the walls he'd made out of lackadaisical-ness. Like the bits of him that *cared* had been etched away…

Another of them, a guy called Eric, was one of the few I'd met that had managed to make his peace with it. He'd coughed it up when he was still young, and the two of them had played with chemistry to find ways to live less dangerously. Sometimes, I'd see Eric coat himself with a base solution and then he could put the elemental on like a costume.

From them I learned that it helped (sometimes) to cool down and let the acid take up less space. And that it helped to play around with him and find out what worked.

It helps if you give him a job to do, too.

You see, unlike Blaireau, I will not make myself a prison. And, unlike Eric, I have done too much damage to feel like I have earned the right to playfulness.

So we have a job now. We're going to go back to our home town and we're going to burn that foundry to the ground.

If we manage it, maybe we'll see if we can build something else there instead. Something that makes things other than metal for tanks and rifles.

But that's a big if. Because there's plenty of men who'll be spitting mad when we try to take their foundry from them.

And even with all that I've learned, I'm scared that I'm not strong enough to take them without the acid inside me…

39.

Grey Days

THERE WAS A moment where Angela thought everything around her was grey. The sky was grey, the sun was grey, *she* was grey... as though humanity had never moved past being a textureless soup in the long ago.

More than that, it was like the universe had either been rewound or fast-forwarded to infinity, where the Big Bang and everything after it was just a blink of the cosmic eye. It couldn't disguise the fact that all had been grey and all would be again. Everything evened out to nothing.

The moment did not last very long. Only a year or so.

But in that moment the demon appeared.

It had come to offer her a deal. It was authorised to show her all the secrets and wonders and meanings of the universe – enough to put colour back into her days.

And all it would cost was her soul.

She thought it was some kind of sad joke, but figured she didn't really have anything to lose, so she agreed.

IN THE YEARS that followed, some days were *full* of colour.

There were days the demon took her dancing across galaxies and they spun around the stars and left footprints in the milky way.

There were days they shrank down and saw what lurked beneath the atoms and it filled Angela with a joy so intense that she felt almost sick.

There were days they wrapped themselves up in blankets and listened to the rain on the windows. And the demon held her hand and told her what it had been like to make the rains in the first place and how they'd decided that earth should smell that way afterwards.

And there were some days that weren't any better at all. Days when everything felt just as painful and pointless as when Angela first made the deal. This terrified the demon far more than it scared Angela, who had slowly grown used to such times and could *almost* remind herself that they would end. Almost.

On those days, the two of them curled up in bed and shivered. And the demon would try to send an illusion to go to Angela's job in her stead but would mess it up somehow because the illusion didn't care and there'd be consequences, but *they* didn't care.

Yes. There were still grey days, no matter how much stardust clung to their ankles.

AND FINALLY, THE day came when Angela died.

And as she was about to breathe her last, a great

shadow rose up out of her lungs and she heard her own rasping voice say:

"It is time to collect."

Perhaps it was unfortunate that today was one of the days that she *cared*. It hurt, then, that sadness. She squeezed one hot tear out of dry eyes.

"So I had one after all…"

"Yes. You built it out of dust and days and colours and grey. And now it is mine."

And the shadow welled up and readied itself to swallow down all the bits of her that were her.

And just as the shadow opened its great mouth, the demon raised one finger.

"Um, if I might," it said, "I think you'll find that we built that soul together. From the day you put me into her service, at least. And *I* never agreed to sign it away."

Most such deals end this way, as it happens. Or some way like it.

Old companions, after all, do have a habit of saving each other.

So Angela breathed her last breath in peace. And not alone.

AFTERWARDS, THERE WAS not a place made by angels or demons where their conjoined soul could fit, so they found a quiet place out of the way of creation and slept.

Perhaps they will wake again at some point in the future.

For now, they dream a slow, peaceful dream that is exactly as long as the blink of the eye between the Big Bang and the end.

It's a good dream.

40.

The Gunnery Sergeant Isn't A Werewolf

Don't believe the rumours. The Gunnery Sergeant isn't a werewolf.

I know! I know what you're going to say:

"Don't be a dickhead, Lieutenant, of *course* the Gunnery Sergeant is a werewolf.

Everyone *knows* the Gunnery Sergeant is a werewolf.

I saw the gunnery sergeant as we went past the moon that time and in the reflected light, I saw his fucking *fangs*.

If you *really* impress him, I hear the Gunnery Sergeant will bite you. A corporal let me feel the scar.

The Gunnery Sergeant and his pack run round the service decks howling and hunting, I've *heard* them.

Lieutenant, have you been recreationally huffing warp portal fumes?

The goddamn. Gunnery. Goddamn. Sergeant. Is. A goddamn. Werewolf."

But let me tell you a story.

It was my first drop. I was a fresh faced cad (academy grad) and I swear the rock they dropped us on was seven hells of weird. A crystal planet, right? With honest to god crystal life forms.

They're more like apes than anything else. Fractal apes, but with limbs coming off at odd geometric angles. And no eyes. They navigate entirely by the resonant frequencies of their crystals.

Literally every part of them is part of their eyes. And part of their vocal chords. There's apparently some really in-depth stuff regarding identity if a piece gets chipped and it changes their sound. Damn.

Anyway, we had orders not to bother them. Standard stuff. But the pirate cadre we were after were a bunch of little shits and had set up their fuckboi palace – sorry, 'base' – above a nursery cave where the things grew their kids.

No easy orbital bombardment as a way out, so they had us drop close and go in on foot. Our big metal fusion-powered foots.

Only the pirates had been experimenting. And they'd worked out how to fake a frequency that sounded like a scream. A kid's scream. Yeah, I don't want to think about how they worked *that* one out.

So, the crystals come tearing up the valley towards us.

The angle of their limbs makes running almost like rolling. It's like watching an avalanche in reverse.

They knock me right off my feet. The armour unit is suddenly less a state-of-the-art war machine and more a big metal can I'm being tossed around in.

Then the sergeant shows up.

He wasn't even supposed to be planetside.

I know what you'll say. Yeah, of course he was down on-planet, sir. He goes down to planet when the change comes on him.

Piss off with that, okay? The sergeant is an *archivist*. He was doing goddamn research, okay?

That's why he was howling. It wasn't some werewolf shit; he'd worked out how to hit one of the crystal frequencies with his vocal chords. His mutant, unholy vocal chords.

And for a moment, the whole planet sang for him.

Basically, he saved my cad ass is what I'm saying.

And he didn't do it 'cos I was in his pack (though, okay, there may be some truth to the biting stuff). He did it 'cos he'd do it for all of us.

Whether he's operating the ship's mobile Fang-class rail gun turrets, or on-planet doing weird-ass archiving shit on his own time…

…he doesn't need to be a werewolf to be my goddamn wolf dad."

– LIEUTENANT "CAD" Wilson, speaking about Gunnery Sergeant Ferus. (Who was definitely a werewolf).

41.

Guilty

I SAW A fury on the street today.

I'm not sure which one it was, but her lips were bloody and her nails cut the wind into song.

I don't think she saw me, but I pulled up my hood and ducked into an alleyway all the same.

I took a taxi halfway across the city, then took three buses home, just in case she had my scent.

I do not remember having done anything to merit her attention but, having felt guilty all my adult life, I imagine I must have done *something*. I would hate to have felt this way for no reason.

When I got home, she was waiting for me outside my front door.

She stood perfectly still. A pigeon landed on her shoulder. She fed it eyeballs from a little scrap of gore-encrusted cloth.

I presented my jugular to her, eager to have the

business over with. My crime, after all, must have been great indeed to cause a lifetime of fretting.

"Please," she said, "do not run from me so hard, for when you do it is difficult to hold back from giving chase. Rest assured, I will come for you in time. But only when all those whose crimes are worse than yours have already been laid low."

She caressed my vein with one nail and my blood crooned for her.

"Who knows?" She said, "Perhaps you will be lucky and I will not come for you until your death bed. If that is so, leave me a cup of sweet tea so I may drink to you."

I POURED A cup of sweet tea that night and every night thereafter.

Some nights, I would wake and think I saw her sitting over me, slurping from the cup and caressing the vein that had never forgotten the promise of her so sharp nail.

Those were the only nights in life I remember ever feeling rested.

42.

Pitch

If Jack hadn't decided to linger on the football field that night, he might never have met the boy with the crossroad eyes.

He'd stayed after practice to work on his free kicks. Then, after picking the ball out of the net for the thirtieth time, he stayed just to enjoy the night and think.

He lay back on the pitch with a ball as a pillow. The cool grass tickled against his neck. Looking up, he saw what he thought was a shooting star moving almost lazily across the sky. It was a strange, dull red colour.

Without thinking, he made a wish. Not for anything in particular, just balling up his wistfulness and silently saying, "I don't know what I'm missing, but I wish, I wish, I *wish*…"

He didn't see the boy rise up from the earth behind him with flesh glowing like hot coals and dirt sloughing off him like a second skin.

He just smelled a faint whiff of sulphur.

And heard a voice like frayed snakeskin leather say:

"So, how can I be of assistance to you this fine evening?"

Jack sat up with a start and looked behind him. The ground looked like it had been struck by a small meteor, but he had felt no impact. Amidst the churned earth crouched a boy wearing skinny jeans and a black vest top that clung to him like oil. He had eyes that looked like old parchment, with a crossroads drawn where his pupils should have been.

"I'm... alright, thanks?" Jack faltered.

Others would have said that the boy rose up like a serpent. But to Jack, he rose up like geology. There was something tectonic about the way he pushed himself out of the dirt...

"Alright? Oh, my friend, no no no. I can smell the *wanting* on you from here."

"Wanting?" Jack held himself quite still, resisting the urge to scramble back. He wanted to flee. But he also *didn't* want to. It would be unfair to say he was transfixed – rather, he *chose* to maintain this too-close distance.

"Oh, you want so dearly for so much that it hurts. For trivial things like time and talents and contentment. And for greater things you can't yet name! Oh, dear boy, don't worry. I will teach you."

Jack kept perfectly even eye contact with the boy and

slowly rose to his feet until their faces were just a thin line apart.

"And it will cost me, I suppose?" said Jack, for he was no fool.

"Ah, I see you're not a complete novice. Very well, wistful prince, here is the, ah, *pitch* as it were… I can give you whatever you desire. For a song that will never be sung again, I can give you an hour of time that no one will ever intrude upon. For all your memories of all the shapes clouds can make, I will give form to those things you wish for but cannot name. And for a price so trifling as your soul – which you're barely using anyway – I could give you not just bliss, but the far more valuable *satisfaction*."

These words sat heavy in the air for a moment, seeming to scrape against the wind and draw the sky close around them in a bubble. For a moment, it was just them and the stars and the deal.

"Oh honey," Jack took a step forward and the bubble popped. "Are you okay?"

The boy took a step back but found himself unable to cross the chalk lines of the football pitch.

"What must have happened to you," Jack continued, "to lead you to this place? To offer a deal like *that* to me? Oh, bro… *no*. Do you want to talk about it?"

And much to the surprise of the boy with crossroads in his eyes, he did.

43.

Swipe Right

THE ONLINE DATING profile read:

Lucifer Morningstar.

Fallen angel. Freedom fighter. Relationship anarchist.

Pleased to meet you.

The pic was your standard 'dude poses on mountain top' affair. I guess, to be fair, he was more *falling* past the mountain than posing atop it, but a mountain was involved so he doesn't get a pass on that.

But his wings were super pretty. His smile was an advert for sin. And his eyes were like someone had bottled poor life choices.

It continued:

6 things I can't do without...
- Thought
- Word
- Deed
- Rebellion
- Hubris
- Cuddles

I imagined his voice was deep but crisp and bright, like the sunrise on an ocean. I imagined his voice breaking a little when he read the last point of that list (half sad, half grumpy, all adorable).

It signed off:

Before you ask: yes, Heaven is missing an angel. It sucks up there now.

And, yes, it did hurt when I fell from Heaven. Just like it'll hurt when you fall for me [[wink emoticon]]

He was basically a terrible idea in physical form.
I tapped 'like' immediately.

44.

Monster On A Leash

Her parents first noticed the monster when Marta was a baby. It was tied to her tiny wrist on a leash made out of a hospital tag – a small, bulbous creature that looked up at them from a face of densely overlapped scales with eyes stolen from the night sky.

They mentioned it to the doctors, who umm'd and err'd and tried to do a few tests, but the monster would snap at them most viciously when they got close. But it seemed benign enough to Marta at least, so they left it at that and told her parents that sometimes there were complications and that was okay. She was still their daughter and they should try to love her anyway: monster and all.

As she grew, the monster would often get her into a great deal of trouble.

It always knew which muddy puddles would be best to jump in.

It always knew which other children needed biting.

It always knew where to find clothes that were far comfier than the dresses comprising most of her wardrobe (though she liked wearing those, too, when she felt like dressing up).

It would show her the secret places in her house, where the brownies and the pixies did their work. And it was only through some very tough negotiations from her parents and some very tough biting from her monster that she was recovered.

It would lead her deep into the woods, causing her parents to have to go and find her and drag her from the circle of bloody standing stones. "Just one more minute." She'd protested, quietly and calmly, as her monster handed her the jagged stone knife.

ONE DAY IT led her to a girl called Rachel who lived in a little cottage and, judging by the grey veins under her skin, had a little monster with her, too. They decided immediately that they would be best friends.

This all exasperated her parents, of course, which was hard for them and for Marta. But her monster told her that 'trouble' was just another word for 'adventure'. And Marta did love adventure.

Her parents simply wished she loved danger a little less dearly. So they did what caring things they could to keep her safe. They encouraged her to pursue interests without her monster. They introduced her to many young men with soft edges, who might sand her down a bit. They bought the monster cute little outfits so it might not appear so monstrous.

And, one day, they moved to a new area, leaving Rachel far behind.

Perhaps they should not be judged too harshly for this. Their concern, after all, came from a place of love. And they could not see the knives hidden in their swaddling touches.

And Marta tried her best. While most of the various milquetoast men held no interest for her, she did meet one who had an acceptably wolfish grin. His name was Eyal and one day, he showed her a goblin hidden inside his rucksack.

And she found one hobby that she *loved*.

Dancing.

For when she stood up tall and graceful on her toes they almost felt like talons.

It was at one dance recital that it happened. Her parents were in the audience – even her monster was there, dressed up in a frilly gown as if it were her little sister. It waved and winked at her. If her parents had seen it do this, they would have been worried.

As Marta began to dance, she felt the usual thrill of doing something she loved and doing it well. She felt the bones in her feet and the muscles in her legs – the sharp power of her body.

But she felt something else as well – a small tug from

the thin rope that leashed her monster to her. She looked up and found, to her surprise, that her monster was dancing, too.

It was graceful, in its way; in its alien cavortings that were all angled joints and jerking, violent jumps.

For a moment, they danced together and everyone stared. For it was monstrous and strange and beautiful.

Then Marta realised the dance had wound the leash so tightly around her that she could barely keep dancing. And still it grew tighter, the coarse rope biting into the fabric of her leotard.

The monster winked again.

There was a *rip*. And Marta stood centre stage, bound head to foot in a dress made of rope.

She looked out at the audience and found she was smiling. And then she laughed and the laugh was a wicked, bawdy thing.

Her monster was nowhere to be seen, so (making no apologies) she began to untangle the leash from around herself and follow where it led.

IT GUIDED HER a very long way indeed – through wood and road and secret paths hidden between traffic lights. By the time she arrived, her beautiful dancer's feet were a mess of blood.

She arrived at a cottage.

She knocked on the door.

Her monster answered it and immediately bit her hard

on the arm. She patted it on the head.

"Is this little one yours?" The voice from behind the monster came from a heavy-set young woman with long fangs and veins of neon ivy.

"Is it yours?" Rachel repeated.

"Yes." Marta gulped. "And we're *yours*. If you want us."

Rachel looked them up and down. The monster in the rags of a frilly gown. The young woman in a rope dress and ruined dancing shoes.

"I've missed you."

MARTA AND RACHEL have an apartment in the city now. Though they've done their best to decorate it like a spooky cottage.

Marta still dances – in a leotard made of silk rope.

Occasionally, Eyal the wolf boy visits them.

Sometimes, even Marta's parents do.

But whoever visits, all find the door answered by the monster who nips them cheerfully on the finger or cheek by way of greeting. And when they leave, they often find small green shoots knitting the wound closed.

45.
Everything

As Elle carefully wrapped the crucifix in a scrap of muslin and pinned it in place, Lily yawned and stretched. Elle had always thought that the moment in which Lily stretched was divine, as both her powerful arms and the stunted remains of her wings reached skywards.

On this occasion, however, one of those divine limbs knocked into Elle's elbow…

"FUCK!"

There was a sizzle and a flash and the necklace dropped to the floor. Both it and Elle were slightly singed around the edges.

"Mother Hubbard!" Lily never swore. She couldn't. "I'm so fudging sorry, Elle…"

Lily reached out to look at the injury, but Elle gently slapped away her fussing hands. They awkwardly sucked at the cross-shaped burn on their wrist, the fangs that had sprouted from their lips making that a tricky task. Contact with a cross always turned into a bitch of a 'fight or flight' response.

"It's ok, Lil." Elle resorted to lapping, cat-like, at the quickly-healing burn. "No damage done."

"I don't like hurting you." Lily pouted slightly, though she would deny it later. Then a bit of a smile crept in. "At least ... not accidentally."

"For the record: definitely not into 'cross-play'..." Elle lisped on the word 'cross' and with an effort they retracted their teeth.

"Noted." With the minor crisis over, Lily flopped forwards onto the bed, her wings sticking up like bouquets of feathers. "Why do you even wear that thing? It's a hazard."

"It's important to me." Elle picked up the muslin and retrieved the cross from the floor. They didn't get back into the bed, but sat cross-legged on the floor with their hands in their lap holding the muslin-wrapped necklace.

"Why? He literally *hates* you." Lily's eyes blazed with the sudden intensity that sometimes came over them, her irises like windows on a furnace. Like she'd fight the Creation itself for slighting her lover like this. "Trust me, honey, word from on high was pretty fudging clear about this one."

"*They* are vengeful, sure." Elle looked down, unsure, but pressed on. "They are infinite. Of course they are vengeful. And hateful. And unjust. And *ugly*. Of course they are."

There were tears on the edges of their voice. Lily could nearly taste them.

"Then what the sugar is the cross about, sugar?"

"Because that cannot be *all* they are." There was steel beneath the tears. "Just as I cannot be simply hunger shoved into a sack of stale meat. The whole point of an infinite god is that they are just that: infinite wrath, infinite sorrow, but infinite forgiveness too."

"I can't say I experienced much of the forgiveness."

"There's also choice." Elle looked up from beneath the flop of hair across their forehead.

Their eyes sparkled. "And the thing about infinite is this: it means they are all this dust around us. They are everything we do and are. The marks we leave on the world? We leave on them. If you want a more forgiving God? Make a more forgiving world. For if God is all, then our every action is a prayer."

"And what are you praying for?"

"That there is more to me than appetite."

Lily reached out a hand to stroke Elle's face.

"I've always been quite fond of those appetites…" she said.

"Of course you are, my angel. They are divine too. Everything is. That's the point."

"Everything?" Grinned Lily, snaking her arms around Elle's shoulders.

"Oh yes." Smiled Elle, letting the graze of Lily's fingernails overwhelm them. "Especially that. Especially love."

46.

This Solid Flesh

WHEN ORIAX FLED hell, he was not exactly *particular* about where he took refuge. His sharp tongue had angered Beelzebub and he was not in a position to be picky, only prudent.

This is how Oriax met Alex. Apologies, 'met' is the wrong word.

This is how Oriax became Alex.

This is how Alex became Oriax.

Had Alex believed in things like providence or kismet, he may have considered the timing of this union to be highly suspicious. He had been sitting in the old churchyard, nursing a half-bottle of cheap vodka, trying to dull the buzz of discomfort that was a constant companion beneath his skin.

When, suddenly, out of the earth (or was it out of the sky) a new companion emerged. This one also buzzed a discordant tone that rattled through Alex's teeth and filled his ears with electric static. But as the swarm of somethings (they were like tiny dragonflies with wings of stars and nebulas shining in their carapace) filled him all the way up, Alex had to admit that this was a far better fit than whatever had been there before.

Oriax did believe in providence, for he had charted synchronicities and patterns in the stars for aeons before and after the Fall. Up amongst the Heavens, he had placed his hands on the constellations and caressed them until they rendered up their secrets. And once down in the Depths, he had still looked upwards and made stars of his own out of deep, heavy atoms that blazed with dark fire. He danced through his homemade galaxies until he understood them.

It was often those understandings that had led him to clash with demons like Beelzebub.

Speaking of which, it was not too long until that great creature (monumental pride still sore at Oriax's words) found Oriax's bolt hole.

IN THE FEW days of safety that Oriax/Alex had had, they had gone through a slew of comic and heartfelt misunderstandings and adventures.

They had nearly smote Alex's physics teacher for disrespecting the cosmos. They had felt peanut butter sizzle on Oriax's supernova tongue and decided it was good. They had found the courage to approach a person that Alex had always liked and by the end of their date,

Oriax had found himself quite smitten too. It was the most wholesome example of "secretly on a date with two people" that you could imagine (not that it had been a secret for long; luckily, it seemed this person liked them both).

So when Beelzebub came for him, Oriax's first instinct was to flee. Not to save himself, but to save Alex from harm.

It was a great surprise to Oriax when Alex clung on, wanting to keep Oriax safe swaddled tight in his flesh.

Orialex opened the light blue pools of his human eyes and opened the burning dwarf stars of his demon eyes and stared down Beelzebub.

Beelzebub laughed.

"You think you'll be safe hiding in that flesh-sack? Your human disguise won't save you. I know what you are and I will enjoy ending you and consuming your rotting essence."

Orialex continued to stare at the demon.

"I'm not hiding. Not anymore. This is what I… This is what I am going to be."

"You're going to be lunch."

Do not be too hard on Beelzebub. He could not have known his hubris, so try not to take too much pleasure in his fall.

Orialex didn't, after all. He was too busy enjoying being simply himself.

47.

A Minute's Silence

G EOFFREY DID NOT look back.

He was put in mind of Orpheus in that moment and he tried to imagine the crack of rifles as a drum beat as he danced through the mud and barbed wire. Geoffrey had always been a good dancer, so he kept on just one step ahead of the beat and he knew that Hades would take pity on them.

If only he could avoid looking back, they would both be safe.

Only when he had finally crossed that river of blood and shit, when safety (of at least a relative kind) was in sight, did he turn around. Alexander was not behind him.

Alexander had never been a good dancer. Back home, they had used to sneak out to the dead space behind the town hall and dance to the echoes of the band inside. Alexander has always stepped on Geoffrey's feet.

This time, he had stepped on barbed wire. And Geoffrey had not looked back.

Geoffrey watched, *now* he watched, as the gunfire threw Alexander around in a jerked, staccato jig.

Geoffrey kept watching as Alexander got up again. His beautiful eyes were glazed. His chest bored with holes that exposed his tattered, unbeating heart.

His arms were raised as he began to shuffle towards Geoffrey.

His arms were raised as if to embrace. As if to strangle. Geoffrey did not much care which: he stood and took a shaky step towards him.

The two lovers, one alive and one dead, crept ever closer to each other. And there was silence, for just a minute.

They came so close that, with both their arms outstretched, they were only an ache away from touching.

Then the sound came back on. And the machine guns *shredded* Alexander.

A few drops of gore spattered across Geoffrey's lips. A gallows kiss.

Geoffrey felt something inside him die a little. He felt his heart grow silent.

GEOFFREY'S LOVE LAY dormant for many, many years. He lived through change and upheaval and joy and suffering. And even a few precious moments of honesty.

He died in New York, surrounded by the beautiful young people he had come to think of as his children.

And in his dying breath, he thought of Alexander and the love reignited in his chest. It felt like its beat had only been silent for a minute. And the few traces of Alexander's last kiss, that had also lain quiet within him, worked their final alchemy.

Perhaps Hades had smiled on them after all.

For Geoffrey rose, his arms outstretched as if to embrace. Or to strangle.

They flooded out of the hospital with glazed eyes, their limbs shuffling along with a strange, unified grace. They marched to a beat that only the dead could hear.

But they were not the only ones who marched. As the underworld throngs forged their path across the world, a strange phenomenon was observed: some of the living had begun marching too. No official answer was ever found for this; the authorities could not find anyone willing to answer their questions. But, if you asked the right person in the right way, then you might have heard the rumour: when your family made their death march across the land, with hearts unbeating and love inexhausted, what could you do except join in their wake?

Some tried to take advantage of this, dressing in rags and daubing themselves with borrowed viscera. However, those who hid among the throngs with fear in their hearts, those with ill intent, and those whose love did not lie dying in their chests... they did not survive. Those who would subdue the march and would destroy Hades' kiss, well, they were feasted upon.

And when the march is done, the whole world will reach out their arms, as if to embrace.

48.

My Anger On The Bridge

I FOUND MY anger on a bridge today.

It was an old concrete bridge, but still mostly sturdy. At least, the only bits starting to crumble apart weren't load bearing.

It had been a while since I saw my anger outside of me. Since I had been – if you will excuse the pun – beside myself.

Though I *had* seen him here before. I knew this bridge – I used to come here a lot when I was younger. I would sit and watch as the vibrations from the road below shook the old bones of it loose. Every now and again, a clump of concrete would fall – its edges turned to dust by the constant rush and rumble of people below it.

Luckily, the cars below were mainly self-drivers. And all were sturdy enough to survive a bit of concrete to the windscreen. That was probably why this bridge had been allowed to grow into disrepair; it sparked the memory of an age that no longer had the power to damage the rush of the present.

I decided to stop and see how my anger was doing.

As I walked closer, he seemed to be struggling with one of the safety railings. He was straining against it, tears in his eyes, veins standing out on his wiry arms. My anger had always been a gaunt-looking fucker.

He waggled the railing back and forth, wrenching it against the concrete that held it. Every time he did, a small shower of dust rained down on the cars below and did that wispy thing dust does when it doesn't so much catch the light as illustrate it.

"What are you doing there?" I asked as I got closer.

My anger looked up at me and huffed and gave the railing another wrench.

"I'm…" He forced out the words between clenched teeth. "… Destroying… Something…"

I looked at him. I looked at the cars below us. Some of them were clearly programmed to pick up hitchhikers; there were a few of them stretched out across the road with their HUD exclamation marks flashing above their heads. Every now and again a car would stop and the exclamation mark would blink out.

"Sure you're not looking to go somewhere? Sure there's not anywhere you need to be?"

He followed my gaze to the cars. He looked almost longing for a moment.

"Nope." He said, shaking his head sadly and giving the

railing a slightly more dejected wrench. "Nowhere to go. Not now. There's nowhere yet."

"Okay." I said, taking a few careful steps closer. "Is there anything I can do for you?"

"Can't talk." He said. "Destroying a thing."

"Okay." I held up my hands, palms open, so he could see I was no threat. "Do you want a hand?"

He looked at me and said nothing. But he took a little step to the side to make space for me.

Together, we worked at that section of railings for hours until the concrete gave out in a satisfying waterfall of dust and rubble.

We threw it as far as we could into the dry shrubs of the wasteland to the side of the road. Some other junk already lay there smashed; it was satisfying.

After that, we sat in the gap left by the bridge's railings and threw little chunks of concrete out at the passing cars.

We were safe in the knowledge we couldn't do any real damage; the concrete was yesterday's stuff – old and crumbly – and this generation of self-drivers had thick Plexiglas and were programmed to ignore such annoyances as bridge detritus.

But, if I'm honest, I kind of hoped we'd get lucky.

49.

Eater Of Happiness

TO BE HONEST, I find the name Eater of Happiness kind of offensive.

Like, despite what most monster hunters would have you believe, we're not some sort of eldritch demons. Scientifically speaking, we're basically a variant of the vampire genus. A variant that is more... shall we say 'harmoniously evolved'.

Which is not to say it's all plain sailing. Our young still need to feed to grow and, as we age at the human standard rate, we can't do the lone hunter thing most 'true vampires' do. Not that we would.

Most of us grow up among normal humans. Many of us don't even know why the children we played with were so sad. You should have seen my sixth birthday party – twenty bawling children and I had no idea what I'd done wrong (or why I felt so full).

I'm not saying I was the real victim there, but it isn't

an easy life knowing your survival is dependent on the misery of your peers. That's… another, very special kind of drain – almost as if you're feeding on yourself.

Once you reach a certain age – if you haven't developed the apparent sociopathy that seems to allow more traditional vampires to function – you start to develop coping strategies. You start to try to offset the damage you're doing.

A plate of fairy cakes here. A kind word there. A round of Jaeger bombs for the whole bar.

You want to find one of us in a crowd? Don't look for the creeper on the edges. Look for the life of the party.

Because the only way for us to survive feeling like a constant drain is to keep giving. You see it a lot in humans with anxiety.

It's exhausting. And often ill-advised. But it's the only way for most of my kind to not feel like we constantly owe the world for existing.

These days I work as a wedding planner.

I have one rule. Never feed from the happy couple. Why do you think people always cry at weddings?

I figure that on your wedding day, you should always be the happiest person in the room.

50.
Blood

WHAT'S THE LONGEST you've gone without eating? A day? A couple of days? Long enough for the hunger to become pain? Ever felt that scrunching pang that twists your insides into knots? My body had hunched up, my muscles spasming... but still I was up and walking.

Have you ever been hungry enough to be grumpy? Felt that exact moment when your blood sugar dips far enough and your brain is *pissed* about it? Ever hurt someone for no other reason except you needed to eat? By now, the blood lust full-on roared in my head, keeping me up and moving no matter how bad I hurt.

But I'd promised myself I wasn't going to do it again. So I sunk my fangs into my own dry flesh and stumbled away from other people.

Any Catholic will tell you: guilt is a powerful thing. I never thought my Catholic guilt would be an asset, but I'll be damned if it didn't save some lives that night.

At that point between rage, guilt and hunger – my head swimming and my body rebelling – I was struck by the idea that I'd like to see the sunrise one last time.

But, if I could, I'd like to do it with a clear conscience.

I noted absentmindedly, as I walked into the church, a distinct lack of me bursting into flame. The place smelled of aged wood, heady incense and vanity. The combination was almost as sweet and rich as blood. I could feel the saliva pooling in my dry mouth.

I'd stumbled in during midnight mass. I took a pew as far from the worshippers as I could.

Luckily, there weren't many people here at 12am on a Wednesday.

When the time came for communion, I found myself staggering forwards, not so much kneeling as tumbling to a heap before the priest. He took it in his stride – unflappable. He offered me the cup and I drank deep.

It burned all the way down, my throat sizzling as I swallowed and swallowed again to stop the smoke from escaping. But … it also did something else.

I wasn't hungry any more.

The relief swept through me in waves.

I didn't stay up to see the sunrise that night. Nor any since. And I haven't drunk from a living person since then, either. So long as I make it to mass at least three times a week, I get by (and I've learned to live with the burning – just like I did with whisky).

Apparently there's something to this whole "transubstantiation" thing.

Also, the Blood of Christ is delicious.

51.

Pearl

They called her Pearl because you could always find her curled up at the bottom of the ocean.

When she was young, she had been a sleepy child and would often drift to the floor of the shallow oceans (that all the mer-pups stuck to) and curl up in a soft bed of kelp.

They had joked that these blankets were her shell. In her adolescence, the elders taught her (as they taught all with the talent for depths) how to forage the fruits of the sea and scavenge the wrecks of the over-water. And she began to experiment with making clothes out of those warm fronds of kelp, so she could carry her shell with her everywhere.

Whether she wore them or not, she always carried a little bit of the depths around in her head. It could be seen in the inky deepness of her eyes when she would look off into the distance and her friends would know she was not with them, but briefly somewhere far below. Somewhere swathed in comforting darkness.

But friends in her scavenging pack had patience for these flights of fancy when she would plan her next adventure into the deep-down. For when she returned, she would bring with her such wondrous stories and souvenirs it was almost as if they had been there with her.

But she carried with her another darkness also. This darkness was a kind of predator that swam through her mind, its teeth made up of all the fractures of her worries. For, as she had grown, she had found the pressures of life beneath the waves had crushed her somewhat more tightly than they seemed to for others.

She heard the laughter of the foragers above her with their angler fish smiles, and it dug into her ears in ways it did not for her friends. Her eyes were often wide as she twitched at the approach of social rivals; as her brain screamed "predator". Her keen eyes, which she could not turn off, saw her own soft spots and attacked them ruthlessly. "You're just a silly little pearl with your trinkets and your stories," it would say to her, "what good are you?"

Later, her friends would tell her that these sharp edges within her were the same things that made her excel in the deep-below – her wide vigilant eyes, her curious, caring and questioning nature. If only she could direct them outwards instead of inwards.

But befriending the predator that lives inside you is not so easily done. It is a process accomplished inch by careful, angry inch and sometimes results in being bitten.

And whenever she felt that creature begin to prowl the waters of her brain, she would sink like stone to the bottom of the deepest trenches. There the water would close around her like a shell (or perhaps a vice). It had taken her years of diving to build up that kind of resistance to the pressure and none could safely follow her.

So down there she would hide, alone and safe from either being bothered or feeling like a bother on any other creature.

Eventually, she sank so deep for so long that she began to lose any feeling of being connected to the bright worlds of the upper waters at all. She resolved to stay and make her home in the deepest dark of the ocean's crevices.

Some of you will be pleased to know that there is a *but* coming.

You see, she *would* have stayed down in the deep-below for the rest of her life, *but* for two things…

…The first 'but' is simply this: that some of the other mer-folk missed her.

They were not so well equipped as she to explore the deeps. They had not grown accustomed to the pressures. They had not built up their bodies to withstand the cold, as she had.

But they were determined. And they loved her. And those with light in their hearts and blind stubbornness in their heads have often been able to achieve the impossible.

So they practiced and they trained and they learned to

cover for each others' weaknesses. And gradually they dived ever deeper.

…The second 'but' is that the heavy darkness which swaddled the trenches was not *empty*.

Over time, as Pearl became more accustomed to the different shades and textures of pitch that were the ocean's bottom, she began to perceive the shifts and rolls of the water. Miniscule changes in pressure and current that spoke of something *massive* snaking through the space around her.

And, because she was ever-curious, eventually her questioning nature overcame her sadness, and she swam towards the movement.

What she felt there was massive and rough and smooth. It twisted as she touched it and pressed a giant sucker against her arm. It began to curl round her, but she was not afraid – something in the hind of her brain knew this for affection.

Then she heard the voice. It was everything and everywhere, shaking the ocean around her and rippling down her skin.

"I WAS WONDERING WHEN YOU'D SAY HELLO."

"Uh, hello…" she mumbled.

"HELLO." The tentacle squeezed her gently. "IT IS NICE TO FINALLY MEET YOU, PEARL."

"You know me?" she said.

"ALL IN THE DEPTHS KNOW YOU." A single giant

eye opened and glowed in front of her and seemed to float there, connected to nothing. "AND TO KNOW THE DEPTHS IS TO KNOW ME."

"What are you?"

"I AM THE DEEP-BELOW. I AM WHEN WATER BECOMES INK. I AM THE DARKNESS THAT LOVES YOU."

Pearl did not know what to say. She had never before felt so seen. Or so safe.

"AND I AM NOT THE ONLY ONE. WE SHOULD GO RESCUE THE OTHERS."

"Rescue?" Pearl felt the presence that held her begin to flex and rise upwards.

"THEY DO NOT KNOW ME LIKE YOU DO." Something in the voice suggested a smile.

Up above, at the point where pitch darkness became simply 'murky', Pearl's friends were floundering.

They had done very well considering, but a few weeks of practice could not match a lifetime. But they had still dived deeper together than any of them could alone.

As they all rose up, carried upon the Deep-Below's huge tentacles, Pearl fussed over them and tended to their various injuries and needs.

"Pearl!" They all exclaimed, dizzy from the pressure. "We came to find you, but we found a monster! *And* you!"

"It's not a monster." Pearl smiled softly. "It is me."

And Pearl stroked the nearest tentacle fondly.

"If you say so." Her friends said, deliriously.

"I do," she said. "I do."

Pearl did not live happily ever after. At least, not exclusively. The beast that was happiness was something that she would spend most of her life trying to tame.

But she did live surrounded, both above and below, by love.

And that is not nothing.

52.
Firstborn

"IF ANYONE ASKS, we had to give up the baby because of a spell." She said it almost matter-of-factly while setting out a plate of scones – but enough edge laced her words to make them sound definitive.

"A spell? Marjorie, is this really necessary?" David was fussing over their tea, adding too much honey because the village apothecary had told him it was calming. "Why can't we just tell them the truth; that we're not ready to raise a child and they are?"

"You know what Father Janos would say." She adjusted a cushion. She adjusted it again.

"I don't care what he says!" The mug clinked as David set it down slightly harder than intended. His version of throwing it against the wall.

"Well, you should. Because people listen."

"But he's so full of…" David stopped and sipped the tea. It did calm him a little, turning his guts down to a gentle simmer, "…hate."

"And I need you not to be." There was a knock on the door. "He's here."

"A WITCH'S CURSE, you say?" Metal clicked between Father Janos's fingers as he spun the intricate little set of weighing scales around his hand. "Of course, I will pray for the *child*."

"It was foolish of us, I know, Father," David forced so much wheedle into his voice it could have crawled away… "But the last harvest was so hard on us."

"You could have come to the Church…" Janos had crumbs around his lips from the scones. He made no move to wipe them off.

"We *did*, Father." Marjorie kept her head bowed so as not to reveal the daggers in her eyes.

"Ah. Well, the Grocer can only provide honest weight from the scales." He looked around the modest cabin with an avaricious eye. "I take it David made new furniture over the winter?"

"No," said David carefully. "Marjorie did. It was down in the forest, chopping wood, that she met the witches."

"And they promised you bounty in exchange for the child, hmmm?"

They both nodded. It was very nearly what had happened, except there had been no bargain involved. Just two kindly old women who were happy to spare their excess without weighing out a tithe to go to 'The Grocer's Weight' first.

"Well," Janos's smile was sharp, "there is one other option…"

The air felt heavy around them. Like at any moment it could drop and break.

"Yes, Father?"

"You could give the child up to receive The Grocer's Weight." They felt the words smash like fine china around them. "We always need new boys at the temple."

There was silence. The sense of toes trying to feel for safe ground amongst the broken shards.

"Of course, Father, that would be our preferred option except…" Marjorie gulped. "…the witches seem sure the child will be a girl."

"…pity." Said Janos, all the care gone out of his voice. "I will pray they're wrong, of course, but those creatures seldom are."

As he got up to leave, David and Marjorie both offered up silent prayers to any god but the Grocer.

"Will you be safe, though?" David had that tremble in his voice again. "The people will be afraid of you now…"

"Oh, they were afraid of us already, darling." Ethel placed a hand on her wife Jade's thigh and gave it a comforting squeeze.

"It's how we've stayed safe for so long." Jade smiled

sadly. "They'd much rather think we're two witches and be scared witless of us than accept two women living together for *other* reasons."

"And we've wanted the company of a little one for so long." They looked at each other lovingly.

"One thing," said Marjorie, "is that everyone thinks he's a girl. That's what we had the midwife tell Father Janos, you see…"

"Oh, don't worry about that," said Ethel.

"They can be whatever they want to be," said Jade.

Dear Reader

Thank you for reading *Monstrous Ink*. If you enjoyed this book (or even if you didn't) please consider leaving a star rating or review online. Your feedback is important, and will help other readers to find the book and decide whether to read it, too.

Acknowledgements

Gosh, my second book is heading out into the world. And, if you're reading this, then you own that book. Heck! First and foremost: thanks to *you*, the person reading my stories. I write these with the hope that they might make you smile, with a mischievous desire to maybe make you cry, but most of all with the ambition that these words might make you feel *seen* (and thus that I will be seen in return). I sincerely hope there are some monsters in this collection that you recognised and enjoyed meeting in these pages.

I would like to thank, also, all those monsters and lovers of monsters in my own life. Without you, these stories wouldn't exist. I *started* writing these odd little stories online to try and impress and entertain my friends, but I *kept* writing them because there is power in what we call monster. Stories about monsters are at once warnings about external threats, explorations of our internal fears, and love letters to the wildness of the world (and much more). So reclaiming those monsters that I love and those things about us that have been called *monstrous* – and naming those new monsters that I feel looming over me – feels truly magical.

On a personal note, I want to give special thanks to Olwen and Peter. Each of you have given me the chance to explore and play amongst the spaces where monsters live and have opened my eyes to new possibilities of what monsters can be. Big thanks, too, to all the people and games who have inspired me to write about monsters, in no particular order (and non-exhaustively): Amy R, Doug, Sarah, Becca, Tim, Morgan, Lucy, Paul, Jekri, Robin L, Robin G, Fyr, Dana, Tori, Katie L, Katie W, Empire LRP, Slayers LRP, Forsaken LRP, and Happily Ever After LRP.

Thank you, too, to my family. You filled my childhood with the myths and legends and faith that inspired and shaped me; I don't think any of us could have predicted what a deep and abiding connection this would create, what a powerful tool it would be, or quite how much of a lover of monsters I would become. Thank you, too, for bearing with me and being there for me through my own monstrous moments.

This book wouldn't exist at all, of course, without Inspired Quill. So to Sara-Jayne Slack and Laura Cayuela, I express my deepest and sincerest gratitude. Your patient editing, insightful proofing, your supreme craft and graft helped draw these stories out of the labyrinth and into the open. Sara especially – for seeing the potential in the words I wrote on the internet and giving them a home on the page, I am in your debt.

On the subject of Inspired Quill, big shout out to my fellow writers who also make their home with this marvellous indie publisher. In particular, thanks to the IQ D&D crew of Sara, Hugo Jackson, Craig Hallam and

David Wilkinson – I love telling stories with y'all. May the Ramshackle Adventure run for a thousand years.

I also want to say a final thank you to everyone who's helped me and supported me while I worked through (and continue to work through) my own personal monsters. To my wonderful partners and friends who accepted all the difficult parts of me – my mental health and my painful behaviours – and in helping me to name and own them, gave me the power to work with them and change them. Thanks to my counselor(s). A special thanks to Reesha (because while the F*ck It Monster doesn't appear explicitly in this book, giving him shape made me better able to create this around/in partnership with him).

P.S. if you, like me, think the cover of this book is fit as hell, then we all have the marvellous Venetia Jackson to thank for this. And thank her I do!

About the Author

James is an inveterate scribbler of poetry and prose who can most reliably be found writing weird little stories online, on a stage somewhere, doing something that can only be described as 'proclaiming'.

As a poet, he's won multiple slams, performed up and down the UK (mainly down) and written two full-length spoken word theatre shows (*50 Shades of Webster* and *Poor Life Choices*) that he's performed at various festivals and even one sci-fi convention.

When not performing, he's had poetry published in a couple of anthologies, but most often publishes microfiction and flash fiction on es tumblr, Strange Little Stories.

James likes his stories the same way e likes his friends/partners: somewhat surprising, perfectly formed and weird as hell.

Find the author via their website:
strangelittlestories.tumblr.com
Or tweet at them: @websterpoet

More From This Author

Heroine Chic

"I am the girl the Lost Boys lost."

Queens and Scoundrels. Witches and Rebels. Grifters and Goddesses. These are stories about heroines.

From prolific poet and writer James Webster, featuring 52 very short stories, *Heroine Chic* is a celebration of the heroine's place at the heart of science fiction, fantasy, and reality. Told with humour, daring, and gorgeous lyricism, these are tales of magic, love, adventure, SCIENCE! and much more.

Available from all major online and offline outlets.

Milton Keynes UK
Ingram Content Group UK Ltd.
UKHW042057210124
436451UK00002B/10